Impressum

Herausgegeben wird die Reihe 10+1 Stories
von Michael Schönauer

Übersetzung Ludmilla Salewski, Bremen
Lektorat Anja Rademacher, Bremen
Titelfoto Ralf Urbschat, Gelting
Covergestaltung Heike Marth, Munkbrarup

Bibliografische Information Der Deutschen Bibliothek
Die Deutsche Bibliothek verzeichnet diese Publikation
in der Deutschen Nationalbibliografie, detaillierte
bibliografische Daten sind im Internet abrufbar
http//dnd.ddb.de

ISBN 978-3-931140-46-5

1.Printauflage 2024

Frank Salewski

Back home — *why?*

KILLROY *media*

The book

The Second World War is over. Eva, the protagonist of the epistolary novel "Back home – why?" is one of the women whose husband has come home from the war and she is unable to oppose him in any way. Unable to cope with his violence and cruelty she confides in her diary. Always striving to keep up the facade for her children and to excuse the strange behaviour of their father, she writes freely in her diary about the disgust and the fear she feels. These diary entries are interrupted by letters to her friend Lilli, in which the author recalls Eva's previous, happy life. Almost unnoticeably Eva's diary entries come together with her letters at the end of World War II to merge into a tragic final chord.

About the author

Frank Salewski was born in 1967 in Schenefeld (Schleswig-Holstein). After completing an apprenticeship as an electrician, the author worked for two years as an electrical mechanic for Lufthansa. He then, as a 23 year old, went back to grammar school and spent his time in the midst of 15-17 year olds. After completing his Abitur (German A-Levels) and reading history and politics at university he completed two years as a student teacher in Braunschweig. His return to Bremen followed and he worked for seven years at a special school for children with behavioural problems. The author has been teaching at a secondary school which focuses on upper secondary education since 2009.

For my Grandma and my Mother in Love

10 + 1 Stories

Band 13, Heimgekehrt
Englische Übersetzung

KILLROY *media*

An Epistolary Novel
by Frank Salewski

Foreword

A suitcase full of letters, one diary and a lot of memories; that was all that remained. Twenty years ago, to the day exactly, my foreman called me to the phone:

"It's for you, it's your father."

It happened without any previous warning. While I thought about the reason of the call, I heard the words of my father as if incidentally.

"Grandma is dead. I'll fetch you in ten minutes."

Grandma is dead.

The words in my head sounded like a never ending echo, until my consciousness rebelled and started fighting against these three words. Ridiculous. Grandma is dead. Absolutely ridiculous. It was only yesterday that I spoke to her on the phone, we arranged to meet on Friday, we wanted to go shopping. Nothing could force me to pass the content of this message to the part of my brain which could comprehend it. Grandma died. A bad dream, I would wake up immediately.

"Frank?"

"What?"

"Everything alright?"

"My grandma is dead!"

It had happened. The truth had found its way out. My brain had outwitted me. The words passed my lips as easily as if someone has asked me for the time. How despicable and insidious is such a brain that it forces me with such a mechanical answer to accept the death of my Grandma in the... in my real world. Verbalized by myself, how could I deny it now?

However, my childish heart and my emotionally controlled mind had not drawn the necessary conclusions yet. How often I have jumped up, driven by the impulse to visit Grandma for a slice of cake or some wonderful fried eggs. But before this thought is put into words or even transposed into action I hear the words again: Grandma is dead. The lovely moments of lightness destroyed; the feeling of youth from a time when the grown-ups were still there, when nobody noticed me much, the important decisions were made by others and everything was put right again with a hot chocolate and a good meal. In these moments I am struck by the knowledge: now you are one of the grown-ups, you are responsible for the hot chocolate and for the solving of problems. Yet can one learn to be a grown-up? Are you born to be one or are you forced to be one because of your biography? And for nearly twenty years I practically had the key to this problem in my hands. I had it from the one person I trusted more than anyone.

After it was obvious that nothing of value was inside no one was interested in the shoebox covered with stickers when we cleared out the flat.

"Only a few old letters and diaries."

But before my uncle could throw the box away like he did with all the other apparently worthless objects, I called:

"Stop, don't throw it away, I want it!"

I added quickly:

"Or is anyone else interested?"

No one was.

At home I made the first and until today the last attempt to sort and understand the content. I took one of the diaries randomly, which consisted of a black, almost fragile exercise book, out of the box and opened it.

"… and how sweet he is, I think I have fallen in love…"

I have never shut a book more quickly. We had only just buried her and suddenly I was met with so much joie de vivre out of these few words. I banished the shoe box into an old suitcase and out of my mind. For twenty years the suitcase eked out a miserable existence in lofts, storerooms or wardrobes, namely my special hideaways, places where it was nearly impossible for me to stumble across it. Probably my childish egoism had not permitted the idea that even my grandma was once young and not only interested in her grandchild to-be.

While I am writing these sentences they appear to me to be like a conspicuously constructed passage of a novel due to the fact that exactly on the twentieth anniversary of Grandma's death the contents of the shoe box became a part of my life and the basis of this book. My wife is responsible for that, for all trinkets are a thorn in her side, just like the boxes containing things I will most probably need some day. That's why my lips were always sealed each time we moved house. I had deliberately taken the suitcase and moved it from one storeroom into the next loft. I knew that I would be able to avoid every discussion about why I had to hold on to a pile of worthless paper.

"It's unbelievable!"

With these words my wife welcomed me home, surrounded by exercise books and letters.

I was speechless; whilst carrying out her inspection of the loft she had managed to get all the way to behind the large wooden beams and had found the suitcase. She assumed that she had found old school things so without hesitation she emptied it. What she had discovered was now piled up on our living room floor. It was neatly sorted into piles of letters and diaries. My wife had done a good job. To my surprise she neither started a discussion about why I kept these papers, nor asked me why I had never told her about the suitcase. The only thing that led to a discussion was my wife's idea to write a book based on the notes of my Grandma. What a strange idea.

Diary entry 25ᵗʰ June 1945

Today was a terrible day. He is back. How long I have yearned for this day, how many dreams wasted for this moment? Always the same image in front of my eyes. Even back then, Christmas 1941, it was not more than an illusion. On his last home leave he stood before me large, broad shouldered and handsome. Unwavering in his belief in the victory and in the job that has to be done. It seemed as if he had managed to preserve the euphoria of the beginning right until that day. Unflappable was his belief in the omnipotence of the Führer. How I would have loved to have been carried away for these 2 days, back into the light heartedness of the year 1933. But how could I?

At first it was nothing more than rumour from Hamburg. Hamburg. Hamburg seems so far away now. The year I lived together with Lilli in the small room behind the shoe shop felt like it happened in another life. Nothing from that is left, nothing, except Lilli. Where could she be now?

Letter from Lilli to Eva 20ᵗʰ December 1941

My dear Eva,

Hans-Georg has to leave for Russia as well now. During his home leave he sold some soap to Mrs Rosenthal, you know, one of our neighbours whose shop was destroyed by the SS in 1938. Whoever watched didn`t hesitate long. The next day we found his marching orders to the Russian front line in our letterbox. On the same day he had to register in Hamburg at his new unit, not as a sergeant, but as private Marten. Enclosed was his demotion because of non-Aryan behaviour and also the order to remove his insignia at once. And I had so been looking forward to a Christmas with Hans.

I wish you a merry Christmas. I hope you have had better news from

Erich.
Please be in touch as soon as possible
Hugs,
Your Lilli

Continuation diary entry 25th June 1945

The rumour about the Jews was true; I already knew, how could I have doubted it any longer? Nevertheless, I could not tell him and spoil these two days. I did not want to destroy his illusion. Maybe it was the first time I was frightened of him. I felt the brutalisation despite all the euphoria. Why should I lie to him? I told him the bronze Mother's cross of honour for our four children was not in the post yet. In the post, what a joke! Until his enlistment, the local section leader, Ranft, had insisted on personally performing the ceremony in the town offices, officially. One year ago I received the first invitation. Four others followed. They always ended with the same sentence: Be proud of the Führer and your fatherland.

Lilli gave me the advice to simply ignore them. Some day they would give it up. I followed her advice, even though she was not the one in danger of running into the local head of office whilst doing the shopping. Hamburg and Quickborn, city and backwater. They're not exactly comparable. Up until now I had been lucky, I only once met Emilie Graber, who had given birth to her fourth child at nearly the same time as me. She asked me whether I had also received an invitation. Unbelievable how quickly she no longer showed any interest as soon as I started to talk about her ceremony.

"Are you looking forward to the ceremony?"

A flood of words followed which didn't seem to stop.

"...my husband cannot come of course... he is doing his duty at the front line for our Führer and fatherland, but he and the whole family are so proud, I cannot decide what to wear..."

As she started talking about the significance of the Führer I said goodbye and congratulated her. I left her with a beaming smile. She had already forgotten about me.

I had never lied to Erich before, even the secrecy of Christmas and birthday presents was difficult for me. I was lucky that the local section leader, Ranft, was already on his way to Russia. He would have told Erich immediately. Lying to Erich's face was not possible. The man who I was attracted to because of his old-fashioned ways and his shyness. It is so long ago.

Letter from Eva to Lilli 8th March 1929

My dear Lilli,

It is such a shame that we cannot work together here in Quickborn. But the shop is really very small. Often I do not actually work in the shop but have to deliver repaired shoes in the surrounding villages or fetch and bring back shoes for a fitting. Mrs Salbei (what a funny name!), who runs this shop for Mr Krause, lives in Hamburg too, right behind the shop in a small room. She is very strict and also tight-fisted. Only to save on the postal charges, I often have to walk hours from one customer to the next. Nearly every evening I have to stay in the shop until nine o'clock to write bills and letters. She says it is part of my apprenticeship and I will need to do it for the examination. Not even on Saturdays am I allowed to go earlier. Father thinks I should count myself lucky that I have such a good job and that it was very friendly of Mr Krause to bring me back from Hamburg to Quickborn so that we can save board and lodgings, now that I can live at home again. It is somehow strange to share a room with my sister. You can imagine that she was not enthusiastic about it. At first Anna did not want to move her clothing from the wardrobe into the chest of drawers. But father said that I had started a career in which I had to look good. He told Anna that as a shop assistant it is important to represent the company and that it would just not be acceptable for my clothes to be creased. He promised to buy her her own wardrobe when she starts learning a profession. He is always so kind. Mother didn't agree with his decision at first; she wanted me to hang up my dresses under the stairs. She also would have never allowed me to go to the Fire Brigade party. Can you imagine? Father asked me if I would like to go with him. What a question! I am going to wear my best dress, the one I am normally only allowed to wear to church. Father agreed to it. I am so excited! Just think, perhaps I will dance with a boy for the first time! Do you remember when we moved our table aside after work to dance? One day we forgot to close the door and suddenly a customer was standing in front of us. I was so embarrassed but you just asked him: "How may I help you?"

I cannot wait for tomorrow! I just hope that Mrs Salbei allows me to leave early. Father wrote a letter to her last week asking for me to be dismissed earlier on this special day. All she said was "What is a seventeen years old girl going to do at a party?" All the same, I hope that she will let me go, for she knows that father and Mr Krause are best friends. I must go to bed now. I hope all is well! Please let me know how everything is in Hamburg.

Love Eva

Letter from Eva to Lilli 9th March 1929

My dear Lilli!

Just this very morning I took a letter for you to the post office and now I am writing again. There is news I have to tell you.

I am so excited I cannot sleep. I have crept out of my room secretly and am now sitting in the kitchen by candlelight. I just hope nobody will wake up and find me here because what I am going to write now is a real secret! I have fallen in love!

His name is Erich and he is so sweet. I think he is older than twenty and is broad shouldered and tall, at least 1.8m. But he is also so shy! The moment we entered the party I noticed him. He was taller than the others with fair hair and was wearing a smart blue suit. I think I stared at him for a long time and when he noticed I looked away immediately. I am afraid I blushed. Fortunately, it was already very crowded. Mother and father were simply occupied with concentrating on not bumping into someone, otherwise Mother would have surely noticed. It was wonderful to be at the party with all the grown-ups.

Of course I mean the Fire Brigade party. I have already written to you about it. I am still terribly excited but I will try to tell you, my dear Lilli, exactly what happened. Mrs Salbei let me leave at six o' clock, so we could go to the party at eight o' clock. As an exception, Mother had prepared the bath today and not tomorrow before church. That's why I could get into the bath when I arrived home and afterwards mother pinned my hair up, I felt like a real lady.

And then at the party, even though it was very full, father noticed a vacant table near the dance floor. He headed straight towards it. But we nearly didn't reach the table, for to do so we had to pass the table of the Ranft family. They're the rich farmers I wrote to you about, the ones who bought a new automobile last year. We could not just pass because father has contact to Mr Ranft concerning business. And once father starts talking to someone, especially to someone who is important to him, he forgets everything else. Mother was very courageous and just said:" Good evening!" and continued straight ahead. I am so proud of her, in these moments she always reminds me a little of you. You are always courageous too.

Anyway, we got the table and father was not annoyed with mother when he came, quite the opposite, I felt he was also proud of mother. Then he ordered a glass of sparkling wine for each of us. One whole glass just for me, just imagine!

We all were in a very good mood and father asked mother to dance with him. I was so elated from the music and was looking forward to the next dance as father had promised to dance with me. Suddenly he stood next to me. I am not quite sure whether he had been standing there for a long time. I only noticed him as he cleared his throat. And then I saw his face, it was bright red. When he started talking I nearly laughed. He spoke like he was out of a novel from the last century, like the ones we used to read to each other.

"My dear lady," he said, "would you do me the honour of dancing with me?"

He also stuttered as he spoke. I think this was the moment I fell in love with him. So tall, so strong and so shy.

Oh I have just heard a noise, I am afraid someone will find me here writing to you. One more thing: he wants to fetch me from the shop when he has a free day to accompany me home. He really did use the word 'accompany'!

I miss you
Eva

Erich declares his love to Eva 30th May 1929

My dearest Eva,

Often I have wanted to proclaim to you, my dearest, a secret that I have held close to my heart and which moves me and unsettles me at the same time. Yet each time I was not brave enough and the words died upon my lips as soon as I was in your uplifting proximity. I can no longer carry this secret with me, my heart is pressing me to confess it to you. For this reason I have reached hesitantly for the quill in order to commit this secret to paper. You may forebode, my lovely Eva, what I want to say. I dare to speak of it openly: for a long time your lovely shape, your beautiful, mild face, your friendly eyes, the soft tone of your dulcet voice, your gentle, precious being have stolen my heart of peace. Your being has taken my mind and thoughts

17

a prisoner and has filled me with sweet, euphoric dreams. There is only space for one thought in my heart now; you, my beloved Eva, to have you for myself entirely. I must acknowledge it: "I love you, yes, beloved Eva, I love you most truly." I hope that you are not too shocked by my frank words.

Yours,

Erich

Continuation diary entry 25th June 1945

Erich is really back. I was completely unprepared. I saw these emaciated figures at the station in their old, worn-out army coats. I saw them get off the trains. Some of them glanced at you angrily, even violently, but most of them seem to be frightened, disorientated. Never could I have thought of Erich as one of them. The handsome Erich as Lilli has always put it. She meant no harm but she was always a bit teasing. She had never understood why one could fall in love with such an old-fashioned man, who, in her words, is not exactly a genius.

Letter from Lilli to Eva 10th January 1930

My dear Eva,

Many thanks for the wonderful New Year's Eve party in your home. Please also thank your father and your mother and give them my regards. Now I have finally become acquainted with your Erich. You are right, he is an impressive man. It is obvious that he has worked hard since his early childhood. You are also right when you say that he is rather old-fashioned. It took nearly 2 hours for him to address me simply as 'Lilli' and not as 'Miss'. At first I thought it was funny, as you had once described it, but it then became cumbersome. I hope you are not annoyed because I was a bit energetic. I think Erich was surprised but not angry. It is said that people from Mecklenburg are always 30 years behind. Nevertheless, Erich has lived here since the age of 15, and even if he has stopped using his dialect, he should learn to talk in a modern way which is fitting with our time. Yet I don't want to speak badly of Erich, I am really glad that you are so happy and that your father agrees with your union. You know, I have always felt drawn to those who are well-educated, those who are more intelligent than I, so I can learn things. And of course to someone with whom I can argue. Maybe someday I will find a suitable husband too.

Love and hugs,
Lilli

Letter from Lilli to Eva 10th March 1930

My dear Eva,

I am very pleased for you that Erich has now got a permanent post at the Ranfts' family farm. Now he can always be with you and must not change the farm all the time depending on harvest times. And with these nice future plans I do not think that it will take long for him to take the next step. You won't believe it; I have taken the next step too. I went out with Hans-Georg yesterday. I had no other chance. He bought two pairs of shoes in the last three weeks in the shop and told me that if I didn't finally go out with him that he would carry on buying shoes until he is bankrupt. He invited me to the cinema and during the film he tried to kiss me. I didn't let him and on the way home we argued about it. I said that this behaviour is not respectable. I also told him of the declaration of love Erich wrote for you and that even after the letter he waited one month before he kissed you for the first time. You must most probably laugh now, Eva, seeing as I made fun of the letter and its style. Didn't I even say that he must have copied it from some book from the last century? And yesterday he was my example for respectable behaviour. Isn't that funny? All the

19

same, Hans-Georg was not impressed, he told me that I am behind
the times and that he has fallen in love with me so why wait? In that
moment I kissed him in broad daylight, I know you would tell me it's
really not appropriate, but I couldn't help it. It was really wonderful.
We want to go out next Saturday again. I am not quite sure but I
think I have fallen a little bit in love. I hope that all is well with you
and your family.
Love and regards,
Your Lilli

Continuation diary entry 25ᵗʰ June 1945

Lilli was right in so many aspects. Later, I found the book from
which he copied the declaration of love in 1929 and another book
from which he had, a year later, copied the letter in which he asked
my father for my hand in marriage. They really were both from the
last century. At that time I didn't care and I still don't today. I loved
his way of dealing with things, his clothing, his language and his
cultivated outward appearance. I loved this man.

And this morning he stood in front of me with a bald head, his face
covered with little scars and abscesses. I had no clue who this
emaciated, stinking figure was. The man, who stood in front of me
had no front teeth and reeked so awfully that I had to take a step
back to stop myself from covering my nose. Isn't it understandable
that I had nearly slammed the door shut: "Sorry we can't give
anything, we don't have anything ourselves."

"Eva."

Everything had changed but the sound of his voice was the same.
Dark, warm despite being slightly fragile. What had I done? I had
treated him like one of those refugees, who hadn't had the luck to
be able to return to a family and a home. One of those who lived off
what they could get by begging on the streets and at front doors. I

had the habit of saying the same words every time. What could I do? I have to feed four children without a husband. Without a husband? I don't know if Erich had even registered my words. I don't think he understood them. I hope for that so much. Now he is sleeping. He didn't even have the energy to wash himself. He staggered directly into our room without a word and then fell onto Marie and Hilde's clean bed with all his clothes on. He slept immediately. He's now been sleeping for three hours. Fortunately, the children are at school again and not home. What will I say to them? They were so proud of their father; they hung on his every word when he told them about the frontline. They won't recognise him. I hope he is still asleep when they come back. I am going to prepare them, to avoid that they will feel disgust when they see him.

Letter from Eva to Lilli 9th April 1930

My dearest Lilli,

I can't believe it; sometimes I really think you must be a clairvoyant. Erich asked me if I want to marry him. Can you believe it? Two weeks after you had written your letter he proposed to me. At first he invited me to the restaurant in Bönningstedt. I was able to order whatever I wanted. I ordered a soup and then a cutlet with potatoes and red cabbage. The dessert was a surprise. It was an ice-cream gateau with a candle in the middle. It was so lovely! And on our way home we made a stop at the Elsensee. We put our bicycles next to a tree and sat down on the edge of the lake. We looked across the lake and suddenly Erich took me by the hand and asked me if I would do him the honour of marrying him. After all this I could not do anything else other than to say yes. It was such a wonderful moment. Erich has talked to father since then but not before he wrote a letter to him, as you will have already guessed. When father received the letter he was strangely concerned, although he assured me that he is very happy for me. And then, after Erich had officially spoken to father, everything was alright. Perhaps he is a bit melancholy because his eldest is going to leave the house so soon. I have never been as excited in my life. There is so much to consider when you're setting up a home. Mother is helping me a great deal. Father has vouched for us and Mr Runge, the owner of the flat, has said we can have Mr and Mrs Müllers flat when they move out in October. We'll have two rooms and a kitchen then. You've seen the flat already; it is the one diagonally below the one of father and mother on the ground floor. At first I was concerned but Erich says we can afford the rent. Erich and father have already decided with the pastor on a date for the wedding. I would have loved to marry during the summer but Erich says we have to have our own flat first. Now the wedding day is 25th November. You are the first person I am inviting. Of course you will get an official invitation too. Are you going to come alone or will you be in male company? If you come alone you can sit next to Erich's cousin, he is the same age as you and seems to be very nice. Everyone is happy; especially my sister is all excited. She often runs after me and shouts:

"Eva Kummer, Eva Kummer!"

She thinks his surname is very funny. Erich and father sometimes look very serious when I see them together but I think it is because they have to consider so many important things.

Love, Eva

Letter from Eva to Lilli 17th June 1930

My dear Lilli,

today was a terrible day, the worst day of my life. I do not know where to start. Everything has changed. You know how happy I have been in the last two months. I already wrote to you and told you how Erich and father sometimes seemed to be worried about something.

I wasn't concerned until I asked Erich what documents we need for the marriage. I hadn't taken care of it because this is, without a doubt, a man's job. Erich surprised me as he told me to ask my father for my birth certificate. When I asked him why he hadn't dealt with it together with the other necessary matters he became a little unfriendly. He told me that I should be the one to ask my father for it. So I asked father for it. After that he became very serious and told Anna and even mother to leave the room.

"Dear Eva", he started and then he couldn't talk anymore, he coughed and became red. He got up and picked up a box from the bedroom and opened it with a key, which he always carries together with his watch on a chain. And then he put my birth certificate on the table. I just wanted to take it and say thank you as the situation was very awkward.

"Open it", was all that father said.

Eva Maria Nagel, born 12th January 1912 in Hamburg Eimsbüttel. I didn't understand, that was my birthday but why wasn't our surname written there? Why not Lohmann? I wanted to say something, wanted to ask father why but then he took two already yellowed newspaper cuttings from the box, each of them an advertisement edged with ink.

Advertisement 25th January 1912
Healthy girl of two weeks of age for sale in Hamburg Eimsbüttel for 30 Reichsmark.
Advertisement 16th February 1912
Healthy girl of five weeks of age to give away in Hamburg Eimsbüttel.

I still did not understand what father wanted to tell me, why he was showing this to me. Then he started to talk. He read the first advertisement in the newspaper and thought it was a joke or a mistake. But after he had read the second advertisement he went to *the newspaper office and asked for the address of the woman in Eimsbüttel. Without asking mother he went to see her and took me with him. From that day on I was his eldest daughter. Father then took me in his arms and I wept and wept. When I had calmed down I wanted to know something about my mother but father just said that she is a dubious person. Actually, I now don't want to know anything more about her at all. Father told me that he informed Erich about my background on the day of his proposal and that Erich insists on visiting her and wants to invite her to our wedding whatever happens. He is in this point uncompromising. He has already found out her address and taken up contact with her. Sunday in one week we are going to visit her. I cannot sleep at night. What should I ask her? How should I address her?*

Dear Lilli, I am so confused. Recently I delivered two pairs of shoes to the wrong customer. Mrs Salbei was very angry. I had to write apologies and hand them over to the customers personally.

I just hope that the next week flies by. If only you could be with me. I miss you

Your Eva

I nearly did not dare to ask you: Do you think we could visit you at your mother's house afterwards? I know that she doesn't live that far away from Mrs Nagel (I can't call her anything else at the moment). Do you think your mother would agree to us interrupting your Sunday visit? I would love to see you.

Letter from Lilli to Eva 25th June 1930

Dear Eva,

You poor thing, I have wished so much happiness for you. I feel your pain. How can a mother do such a thing? What a trial for a child. I dare to say it, in my opinion it is a mistake to visit such a person.

There may be reasons which lead a young woman to give a child away but there are state-institutions for these kinds of problems. It is not excusable to expose a child to such a danger like this woman has done. One needs to be deeply thankful for your father. I truly admire his courage. I am sorry for my direct words and I do not want to question the intention of your husband to-be too much but please prepare yourself when you visit this woman.

As for the visit at my mother's, dear Eva, I must tell you off. You know that she always was happy when you accompanied me on my Sunday visits! She really thinks highly of you. I have already told her about your engagement and I think she would love to get to know your husband to-be as well. But please try to turn up before seven o'clock because I have to be off then. You know that Mr Krause is not happy to see one of his girls on the street after nine o'clock. And the elderly Mrs Lemmermann still lives above the shop and reports everything back to Mr Krause.

I hope to see you on Sunday

Hugs,

Lilli

Letter from Eva to Lilli 30ᵗʰ June 1930

My dear Lilli,

Sadly, I couldn't visit you on Sunday. It was not a matter of time as Erich had borrowed the old automobile of the Ranfts family. It would have been possible for us to have been on time at your mothers. Yet Erich thought it was unsuitable to visit an (to him) unknown woman in her home, especially when I can't avoid talking about matters concerning the family. I would have loved to have seen you to tell you everything. So I have to tell you the news via this letter. I was so excited. I wasn't able to say a word during the trip. Perhaps it was a good thing, for Erich was very serious. He looked nearly strained. He never looked at me. When we arrived I wasn't allowed to get out of the car. Erich said it's not appropriate. A woman has to wait until the man has opened her door. At first we had to go into a backyard. We had to ask a young man to help us find the way. There weren't any house numbers. The young man told us to take the outdoor stairs to the first floor and knock on the first door. I felt uneasy because the way led us through two houses. It was very narrow and despite the midday hour you couldn't see anything. Without Erich I would never have gone this way. When we arrived in the backyard it brightened up a little bit. As we walked up the creaking stairs I thought they were going to collapse. Erich knocked but as we heard a "Come in!" he pushed me through the door. "It is your mother," he muttered.

Then I saw her. Mrs Nagel is a very fat woman who was sitting in a broken armchair. Just imagine, her chamber pot stood on a small table directly next to the armchair. It smelt a bit unpleasant too. When she saw us she laughed and said: "You must be Eva, take a seat on the bed." I sat down on the bed but Erich preferred to stand. Erich said that she, as my real mother, has to be present at our wedding ceremony. The woman answered that she would love to come but that it is not possible because she hasn't got a dress and no money for the trip. Erich then gave her a lot of money, two weeks wages. Before we left I had to give her my address, for she wanted to write her daughter a letter before the wedding, as it is so far away. We said goodbye and she took my hand, pulled me down and kissed me on the cheek. It was really very unpleasant. On our way back Erich was happy. He didn't want to visit you but he talked a great deal more to me. He said what a nice meeting it was and what a reasonable woman my mother is. All I thought was that she is not my mother but I held my tongue. I didn't want to spoil his good mood. I told father later and told him that he is my father and mother my mother. He took me into his arms and said "I know".

I plan to not think about it anymore and to look forward to the wedding. There is still so much to prepare.
I am looking forward to finally seeing you then.
Love,
Eva

Letter from Mrs Nagel to Eva 17th July 1930

My dear daughter,
It was touching to see you and your husband. I was glad that you are a pretty girl. You look like I did at your age. Your husband is also very remarkable, as a young girl I would have liked him too. The money is already all gone, I spent everything on a dress. So I need some more money for shoes and the fare. Perhaps the same sum again. You cannot expect me to afford it on my own. Please send the money to me so I can come to your wedding too.
Your loving mother

Letter from Eva to Lilli 20th July 1930

Dear Lilli,
I quarreled for the first time with Erich yesterday. Because of my...because of Mrs Nagel. Just imagine, she wrote me a letter and asked for more money so that she can come to the wedding. I showed the letter to Erich and he really wanted to send her the money. I didn't want to and said that she will not be coming to my wedding. Erich kept repeatedly saying that a mother has to go to her daughter's wedding and that's the way it should be and that blood is thicker than water. I was really distressed but he wouldn't listen to me. So I went to father. He told me that I have to clarify such things with Erich alone now but he still talked to him. Erich came and said that he agrees to her not coming to the wedding but I have to promise to correspond with her. He really used this word. I promised but I think

27

that if I do not send her any more money that she will stop writing back. Erich is still somehow in a bad mood, I think it is because I talked to father. He hasn't said anything about it though. Anyway, by the time the wedding day comes everything will be better. I am so glad that this woman won't be coming to my wedding. The only thing that makes it a little sad is that you haven't seen this immensely fat woman, we could have laughed about her nicely. It's good that Erich can't read these lines.

I am happy that we will be seeing each other soon.
Your Eva

Letter from Lilli to Eva 12th January 1931

Dear Eva,

You've only just married and already I have news; Hans-Georg and I want to marry too. I don't think I will find another man with whom I can argue and then make up with like I can with him. So I asked him, when are we going to marry? And you know, he wasn't shocked at all but rather said that we will marry in April. I looked at him and was a bit shocked myself, that's very soon I thought. But I didn't say anything, you know me. And now we are going to marry in April. Next week we are going to talk to the pastor to set a date. I will let you know immediately. I hope you are well.

A loving hug from your slightly nervous
Lilli

Letter from Eva to Lilli 16th January 1931

Dear Lilli,

I was so happy when I read your letter. You are going to be married too. I think I may be more excited than you. Honestly, how could you just ask Hans-Georg? Erich would have been deeply offended and would have turned his back on me. But that is what you're like! It

serves you right that Hans-Georg hasn't let himself be put off. You are right; he is the right man for you. I am so happy for you.
Looking forward to your wedding
Your Eva

Letter from Eva to Lilli 10th June 1931

Dear Lilli,

Sadly we haven't seen each other since your wedding to Hans-Georg. That was two months ago. Since then a great deal has happened. Can you believe it, I am four months pregnant! That's why I didn't drink alcohol at your wedding. It is not at all like everyone says, I haven't been sick once in the past months. It is the exact opposite, I feel on top of the world! And people are right when they say you are hungry all the time. Now that the third month is over I can tell our neighbours. They always teased me and asked when they will hear the tapping of baby feet in our flat. I wasn't bothered at all but Erich sometimes became very angry when I told him about it. "They ought to mind their own business!" he said. Yes and after I was pregnant he wanted to tell the neighbours at once but I wouldn't let him. During the first three months a lot can go wrong. Now, seeing as I am in the fourth month, Erich is taking every opportunity to tell the neighbours and friends the good news. He even borrowed some sugar from the Schmidts' although we had enough, just to let them know. Often he brings an extra litre of milk with him from the Ranfts'. "For my son and heir", he always says. He seems to be sure that we will have a little boy. I don't think about it. I just hope we have a healthy child and (I only dare to say this to you) I am a little bit afraid of the delivery. I know that my mother always says such a birth is no problem and even the doctor says that I am as fit as a fiddle and in addition to that that I have a wide pelvis. In spite of everything I am feeling quite uneasy.

Do you think I am silly, like you did back then when you laughed at me because I was afraid Mr Krause could come into the shop and catch us chatting? I believe that a leopard can't change its spots. What about you? Do you like married life? Do you want children too? Is Hans-Georg well and has he got the job as authorized signatory at his company?

Now I have to say good-bye, I have to go to the Ranfts', they have allowed me to collect a bag of potatoes from one of their harvested fields.

This evening I'm going to cook boiled potatoes with linseed oil for Erich. He loves to eat the skin of the potatoes. If I hurry up there will be enough time to prepare a bath for him before he arrives home. He always says a daily bath is the only luxury that is important to him. I can only tell you this; I think Erich is slightly vain.

I miss you, please write soon

Your Eva

Letter from Lilli to Eva 27th June 1931

Dear Eva,

I was very glad to hear from you. I'm pleased that everything is well. Your pregnancy is really a wonderful surprise. A lot of responsibility awaits you now. My dear Eva, whether I think you are silly? Yes, but only if you think I can't understand your fear of the delivery. Of course, even a birth today is somehow dangerous and even if no woman talks about the pain that does not mean there is none. My mom always said it's better not talk about it, otherwise no woman would give birth to a child voluntarily. That shouldn't discourage you, on the contrary, you know I think it is right if you know what you are letting yourself in for. I had to smile a bit when I read that Erich is sure about the fact that you will have a boy. Hopefully he won't be disappointed.

I can tell you that I am not pregnant yet and we try to take all precautions so that it won't happen. Of course you can't be perfectly sure that it will work. Anyway, we hope we are lucky. Up until now no one has asked me about my state apart from great-aunt Frieda. In the city it is different, we seldom see our neighbours and when we see them we only say "Good afternoon". Hans- Georg is teaching me to write on a typewriter and if I carry on doing so well I think I could perhaps start next month as a typist in the company of a business friend of Hans-Georg. Mr Krause will have to look for someone else in his shop if this is the case. Maybe, if Hans could teach me some more bookkeeping (more than the accounting of Mr Krause's records) I could become a secretary someday. With Hans working as an authorized signatory and if I get a better paid post, we may open our own little shop in three years. You know that that was always my dream.

Hans and I are getting on with each other well, even though we still argue a lot, which is no news for you.

Love,

Your Lilli

Postcard from Erich to Lilli 20th November 1931

Dear Family Marten,

Today I have a very happy message for you. Yesterday evening at ten o'clock I became the father of a strong, healthy girl. Despite the restlessness, the little addition to the human race fills our home with an indescribable happiness. Mother and child are in good health.

Yours sincerely

Erich Kummer

Letter from Eva to Lilli 25th November 1931

Dear Lilli,

Today I got up for the first time after a longer period of time after the birth and I really feel the need to write to you. I am so happy that Marie is a healthy child. She is really sweet, even though her head still looks like an egg. The doctor says this is quite normal. I am still exhausted even though the delivery didn't take too long. The pain was really terrible. However, I think your mother is wrong. Maybe she was joking when she said that because this little human being was worth every effort and all the pain. You were surely surprised because of Erich's postcard but I couldn't stop him writing one to you too. He says this is the way it should be. Of course he consulted his book from the last century. I had to write the addresses of all members of the family and friends on the postcards weeks before the birth. He even sent one to mother and father although we live in the same house. That's the way he is, everything has to be in order. He was also a little disappointed when he heard that I gave birth to a girl but after the neighbours cheered him up and told him the next one will be a boy he is now happy. He even carries her in his arms and runs around with her. But he doesn't change her nappies, he says this is a woman's job. And I think he is right. After all, he works the whole day and I stay at home to care for Marie. I am looking forward to see you at the christening. I hope you can come? I have already spoken to Erich about it and we think you should be the godmother. At first he disagreed. He said that the godparents ought to be from the family. So I told him that you are like a sister to me and then he approved of it. The second godparent will be his uncle Max. You know the one who sang the little song at the wedding? We want to talk to the pastor tomorrow to fix a date for the christening of our little Marie.

I hope all is well, my regards to Hans-Georg

I hope we will see each other soon,

Your Eva

Letter from Lilli to Eva 10th January 1933

Dear Eva,

Now it is a little over a year ago that I held Marie as her godmother above the font and in two weeks your Hilde will be christened. I am so glad that your second pregnancy and birth went even better than the first. You can be thankful that you are able to cope with the housekeeping and the two children only two days after the delivery. It is such a shame that your mother is ill at this time. She was such a good help with Marie. I wish her all the best. It is touching to hear how your father is caring for your mother and is still trying to help you as well. Sometimes I am envious of him, you know, because my father was killed in action in 1917 and I haven't got any memories of him.

I would have loved to help you too but, as you already know, because I am now a secretary, I won't have any holiday. Sadly we can't come to the christening of Hildchen for the same reason. They expect me to work late on Saturdays. Even the last three Sundays I stayed in the factory. Mr Burmeister, the owner of the company, said it is important for my professional development. It is really exhausting. At least there is one positive point: Now Hans-Georg knows what it is like to be alone on a Sunday. I think I have written to you about this topic more than once and about that we have argued about it again and again. Last Sunday he asked me on which Sunday I would eventually spend a day at home. At first we quarreled again but then we had to laugh and we made up again. The following lines are somehow difficult for me but I can't help but write them. It must have been really painful for you that Erich wasn't happy about the birth of Hilde. You held your tongue but I know you. You can believe that I was ready to drive to him to tell him my opinion. But luckily Hans held me back. You know he is more level-headed than me. He had a serious talk with me and told me it is a very difficult situation for

Erich. Naturally, I didn't want to listen at first. I was really angry. Yet after a while I recognized the truth in his words. He said Erich was educated in an old-fashioned way with the traditions before the war and there are a lot of people who think the same, especially in the country regions. Maybe he is right but in my opinion it is not right. Even if it was this old-fashioned style which made you take him. Don't worry too much, he's grown very fond of Marie with time.

I enclose some money as a present for the christening. I know you can make good use of it. I know Erich is too proud for that kind of thing but just tell him that this way we save on the postage costs of a present. He will understand then. He always says you should not give presents. The small amulet I enclose is for Hildchen, so that she has something when times are worse. This could happen faster than we think.

I miss you and am thinking of you!
Hugs, Lilli

Diary entry 27th June 1945

It is twenty to five; I cannot sleep any longer so I'm using the time before I have to make breakfast for the children to write. Yesterday, the encounter with Erich and the children went well. I fetched them from school. Erich was sleeping deeply so I decided to leave him alone for a short time. At first I didn't know what to say. Then I simply told the children that their father is back from the war but that he is very ill. I prepared them for the fact that they won't recognise him and that he will recover after some time. The little ones believed me, for them it was like an adventure when they saw him lying on the bed. I am not quite sure about Marie and Hilde, they cried. Erich did not wake when they spoke quietly to him so I took them into the kitchen. Yesterday, I put it off but when the girls return from school I will have to tell them. There is no other way. I have to tell them why they must sleep with me in one bed for the coming time. I am going to say that their father is so weak that he needs a bed of his own to be able to recover from his illness. They will understand. They are so sensible. I cannot tell them the truth; that I don't want to sleep in the same bed with Erich. How could I tell them that? How could I say that I feel disgust for their father? I can hear the children getting up now.

Continuation diary entry 27th June 1945

Finally the children are asleep. I crept out of the room. Erich wouldn't really wake up this morning. I planned to prepare a bath for him, even though it is Wednesday, but he hardly recognised me. I don't think he even knew where he was. At first I didn't want to touch his forehead to check his temperature, for I was afraid one of the abscesses could burst. And when I did in the end he felt very hot. He opened his eyes and I noticed how glazed they were. I sent Hildchen to the old doctor, Mr Schnell, at once. He is nearly eighty years old but because his son has to work in the English military hospital, he is practicing medicine again. He came in the afternoon. He said Erich's condition is alarming; he is suffering from a serious infection and is too thin. He also told me that the nasty smell is a result of the open sores and that I must take off his clothes and wash him. I have to wash out the open wounds repeatedly every day with chamomile. This is the only medicine that is still available in great quantities. I don't know how to thank Doctor Schnell for his help. He didn't want to be paid and when he left he gave the children some chocolate. He said he has more because his son gets special rations from the English. This evening I started the task of washing Erich, I sent the children outside beforehand. After the first effort it went quite well but it is terrible to see Erich in this condition. In times past I would have never been able to roll this tall man from one side to the other. Today it was so easy. Erich didn't wake up, he just groaned when I washed out the open abscesses. I have got the feeling that he is sleeping more peacefully now. I don't know where I am going to get the solid food from which the doctor has prescribed for Erich. I've got nothing to exchange. I buried our silver in the Ranfts' chicken coop but they said that the English looked there first. For the chocolate, which I had to take away from the children, I won't get enough to cook a strong broth. At the most I'll get a few potatoes. There is only one thing left, the amulet that Lilli gave Hildchen in 1933 for her christening. Such a treasure around the neck of a twelve-year old girl. It is pure gold. Lilli said that she will always have something for emergencies. In 1933 I never thought of the bad times to come.

Letter from Eva to Lilli 7th February 1933

Dear Lilli,

You have once more gone over the top, what a treasure you gave our Hildchen. An amulet made out of pure gold for bad times. You really are unbelievable. I am so happy to have you as an aunt for my children. Isn't it sheer luck what is happening around us? Germany is an important country again. Mr Hitler is really a significant person. When we heard of the appointment of Mr Hitler as the Chancellor of the Reich Erich and I invited the neighbours to our flat. Everyone in our village celebrated and in the evening more than one hundred men went singing through the streets waving flags. It was almost like a village party. Everyone is talking about the Führer now, even Erich calls him that. You have often written that you and Hans-Georg don't like Mr Hitler but I think that you have probably changed your mind now. What can be wrong with Germany showing France that we won't put up with everything. After all, the French did shoot your father.

KILLROY-Künstlerroman
Torsten van de Sand – Robertos endlose Reise

Was wäre geschehen, wenn Bob Dylan nicht im 20./21. Jahrhundert gelebt hätte, sondern im Italien der Renaissance?

Robertos endlose Reise erzählt die Geschichte des Sängers Roberto di Lane, der 1478 wie aus dem Nichts in Florenz auftaucht und aufgrund seiner kraftvollen, originellen Lieder schnell bekannt wird. Er begegnet den Großen der Renaissance und befreundet sich mit Botticelli, Michelangelo und Leonardo da Vinci. Er findet den Ruhm, den er sich ersehnt, und droht daran zu scheitern.

Auf seinen Reisen ist er stets in Gefahr, ein Spielball politischer Machtkämpfe zu werden. Angetrieben von seinem kreativen Genius und der Suche nach Grenzerweiterungen, findet er einen Weg, seine Kunst zu leben. Diese führt ihn kreuz und quer durch Italien. Vor dem Hintergrund einer Zeit des Wandels entfaltet sich ein imposantes Renaissance-Roadmovie. *»Nichts ist neu. Alles kehrt wieder seit Tausenden von Jahren.«*

**Torsten van de Sand
Robertos endlose Reise**
Künstlerroman
584 Seiten gebunden,
28,00 €
ISBN 978-3-931140-44-1

KILLROY media® · www.killroy-media.de

What about your efforts to start a shop on your own? Has the owner of the delicatessen shop finally decided whether he wants to sell it to you both? I am really very excited. You are going to fulfill your dream at last. Just think, if the shop is successful then you can hire an apprentice. I wish you all the best!
Kindest regards,
Your Eva

Letter from Lilli to Eva 11th February 1933
Dear Eva,

I've got great news for you. Hans-Georg and I are going to be the new owners of the delicatessen shop soon. Mr Schumacher came personally last Saturday and promised to sell us his shop. However, not exactly for the price that Hans-Georg and I were expecting. Mr Schumacher will only sell the shop to us if we take over the outstanding accounts. They mainly consist of outstanding bills belonging to important persons, as Mr Schumacher called them. These are customers whom Mr Schumacher granted a loan because of their name or wealth. He was very honest and told us that in terms of getting the money back that it is only a question of time. With the ones who only have a good reputation, there could be a few problems. We accepted, although our savings are not enough so we will have to borrow some money from the bank. Hans and I agree on the fact that as long as we are in debt that I will continue to work as a secretary. We will be busy with the orders and account books after work and on the Sundays that I don't have to be at the company. We will also take care of the cleaning of the shop ourselves. On the days the goods are delivered Mr Schumacher had a temporary helper, Mrs Meier, a nice pensioner. We want to continue this tradition. She will support Hans at the beginning. We are going to try and slowly reorganise the shop and change it from a delicatessen shop into a grocery shop for everyone with a delicatessen section. Step by step. It is important not to annoy the old customers and still attract new customers.

The election of Mr Hitler as chancellor of the Reich really worries Hans and me a lot. On the evening that you celebrated some of his supporters went through the streets of Hamburg and beat up people who were not followers. This is nothing new; in the last few months the supporters of Hitler have been attacking political opponents. Concerning my father; he probably also shot French soldiers before his death; otherwise he wouldn't have received a medal for bravery. I don't know who started this war. I just know that people kill each other in a war and that that cannot be right and if another war breaks out now that it will be due to Mr Hitler. I just hope that it will not go that far.

Hugs,

Lilli

Letter from Eva to Lilli 19th February 1933

Dear Lilli,

I don't want to argue about politics with you. If I'm honest I don't understand much of it. I rather keep out of these things. Erich, on the other hand, is really enthusiastic. He joined the NSDAP last week. He wanted me to join also but I don't think much of being a member of a political party. Father agrees, he says we have to wait and see what happens next with Mr Hitler. I think without Father Erich would have pressured me further to become a member of the party. What I like are the evening meetings of the comradeship, which take place every second Saturday. Often they are in Mr Ranft's barn. He is very enthusiastic. I don't care why we meet, it is an opportunity to go out and every time we receive a free drink. We sing together, which is really nice; it reminds me of the evenings when father took out his accordion and we sang together. I am not interested in the speeches which are held every time. I sit together with the other women and chat. Sometimes we teach each other new knitting patterns. Lately, Erich has been wearing the uniform of the party in his free time. He was one of the first who became a member of the party after the election and so the uniform was paid for by Mr Ranft. I must say he looks pretty handsome.

Your news of the shop is really great; I am a bit envious of it. I just hope the shop and the post as a secretary won't be too much for you. You have already told me how exhausting it is. Nevertheless, Hans-Georg will help you. I am so excited. Erich has promised that we will visit you when everything is in order. I think he will be able to borrow Mr Ranft's automobile again. I am so curious to see your shop.

Can you imagine that little Anna is engaged. My little sister is going to marry. Sadly, mother is very ill but this news got her on her feet again. She is changing my wedding dress at the moment. Anna is the fourth to marry in this dress after grandma, mother and me.

Now I have to tell you something sad; Mrs Nagel died. I received a letter from her neighbour. She found Erich's letter and the one I wrote to her after the wedding. She says she lay in her bed and passed away peacefully. I will not be going to the funeral. Erich disagreed but I'm still not going to go. That's why Erich put an obituary in the newspaper in Hamburg. It is a strange feeling to be honest, I'm not really sure if I am actually sad. I feel sorry for her, especially when I see my little ones. She never had the feeling of happiness to see your children growing up, although she had the opportunity. And she cannot enjoy this lovely spring.

I hope everything is alright and that you will find some time to write soon.

Hugs
Your Eva

Obituary Clara Nagel

> *Mrs Clara Nagel passed away on 15th February 1933 in Hamburg at the age of 57.*
>
> *Gone but never forgotten.*
> *Erich Kummer and*
> *Eva Kummer (née Nagel)*

Letter from Lilli to Eva 22nd February 1933

Dear Eva,

It is sad, of course, that Mrs Nagel died. Maybe on the other hand it is good for you. This unwanted episode is finally over.

Yesterday was an exciting day: Hans-Georg and I went to the notary. Hans signed the contract of sale. I took an extra day off just for this event. After sorting the formalities Mr Schumacher drove with us to the shop and gave us the key. Afterwards we took a bottle of sparkling wine, one for two Marks, from the shelf and raised our glasses. Mr Schumacher gave us the advice not to change the name of the shop too early. We are going to keep the name "Jakobus Delicatessen Shop". Mr Jakobus founded this shop more than fifty years ago. Tradition is very important for the customers, said Mr Schumacher, that's why he never put his name above the shop. I think it is a bit sad but this way we'll save the money for a new sign. From now you can visit us every Sunday because I think we will be very busy and won't be able to visit you. I'm looking forward to showing you the shop. If it is possible please call me from a telephone beforehand. You have got the number already. If I say: "I'm sorry, you have been connected to the wrong person", you know Mr Burmeister is present. Please try again later then.

Dear Eva, I'm very happy about the fact that you haven't joined the NSDAP like so many others. You have to be really careful with this

party. Everywhere you hear stories about dismissed civil servants who
disagreed with Hitler's ideas. Especially the Jews are having trouble
with the party. Mr Hitler has cursed and sworn about them during
the election campaign. Hans-Georg fears even worse things will
happen. I hope people will use their common sense again. Everything
will calm down when everyday routine returns, just like in Quickborn.
A wedding in your family again. What a surprise. I'm glad to hear
your mother is distracted from her suffering by the upcoming
wedding. Often occupation is the best remedy. Perhaps you will
become an aunt soon and then your two children have someone to
play with. Tomorrow will be a very exciting day, the former employees
and business friends of Hans are going to visit our shop. I've already
prepared cold platters. However, I won't be able to attend. Mr
Burmeister said he couldn't allow for me to have another day off, even
though he is invited too. I'm looking forward to the day when we have
paid off all of our debts and I won't have to go the office anymore. If
we live modestly and the shop carries on running like the last few
months, according to the account books, I will be able to give up the
position as a secretary. Now I have to go to sleep, Hans-Georg is
already fast asleep.
Love,
Your Lilli

Diary entry 28th June 1945

I feel terrible. When the children wake up I have to talk to
Hildchen. Yesterday, I postponed it, hoping for some kind of
miracle. But there wasn't one. Sadly I didn't get as many potatoes
for the chocolate as I had hoped. I will tell her that I need her
christening present in order to prepare a really good meal for her
father. I hope so much that this sacrifice is not in vain. Yesterday
the doctor came again to see Erich. He shook his head indiscernibly

when he examined him. I saw it. When he turned around I saw the concern in his eyes. I don't think he has much hope for Erich. I still don't want to give up. I will go to the black market with the amulet today.

Continuation diary entry 28th June 1945

Today the little miracle that I hoped so badly for happened. Hildchen said that she is not sad at all, the health of her father is far more important. I'm quite proud of her. As soon as the children were on their way to school I was on my way to the market. It is unbelievable what you can get there seeing as the shops are nearly empty. I stopped at the first stall where a woman was selling two chickens and a piece of meat. I was nearly in agreement with her; I was going to get half a chicken and a piece of the meat for the amulet. At the exact moment that she wanted to cut the meat a hand pulled me backwards. I was so frightened! I naturally thought the English police would take me away with them. Thank goodness it was the son of Mr Ranft, who was sent to England in 1934 by his father.

"Aren't you Eva Kummer, the wife of Erich Kummer?" he asked me. He recognised me of course, it hadn't been long since the evenings at his father's farm. He was already grown up back then. Without asking me he told the woman with the chickens that it unfortunately was not a deal. And then he took me to the farm. For the amulet he gave me one whole chicken and a good piece of salted pork and different sorts of vegetables. He promised me that when the times are better and if he hasn't been forced by then to sell the piece of jewellery that I could buy it back from him. I was so happy when I returned home. I wanted to cook a great stew for Erich but he sadly hadn't managed to use the provided bucket. So first of all I had to clean up his bed. What luck that we received so much bed linen at our wedding. Although I had the windows open the whole day, the penetrating smell is everywhere, even in the kitchen. We can only be pleased that it is summer! How could I heat a room with open windows? Winter is still a long time away and hopefully it will be better then.

I managed to make him drink a cup of broth. I think it was good for him, although he is still not talking with us. He also does not feel so hot anymore. For the little ones it is a great strain. During the day they don't like to be in our room. They sit in the kitchen or play in the street. Concerning the big girls I have other worries. Although the English are not allowed to have contact to us Marie came home today chewing gum. When I asked her she assured me that all the girls in her class ran into some English soldiers after school. They just tried to talk to them. As they are learning English at school some of the girls tried some English phrases. But they didn't listen. When parting they gave each girl a piece of chewing gum. I am still concerned. Marie is a very pretty girl and the soldiers are very young. She looks for her nearly fourteen years like a grown-up. Luckily I don't need to worry about Hilde, for she is a real bookworm. My old teacher Mr Brabant, always lends her new books. She reads very difficult books like Goethe and Schiller and even two books by the famous Englishman, who wrote everything in verse. She is also very belligerent and boys would be afraid of her, she does not put up with anything. She almost reminds me of Lilli.

Letter from Eva to Lilli 28th February 1933

Dear Lilli,

I am so sorry about what happened on Sunday. Everything started so harmoniously. I enjoyed the trip to you in the automobile very much. The weather was just wonderful. I had the window open the whole trip. It was such a nice feeling to put my arm into the wind. Even

Erich was in a good mood. It didn't take long to persuade him to wear a private suit and not his uniform. We even sang together. It was so much nicer than our last trip to Hamburg. And your shop! It was much bigger and nicer than I had imagined. I was so proud of you. And even Hans-Georg and Erich seemed to get along with each other well. If only Erich hadn't seen the sign in the corner. Flowers from Friedhelm Rosenthal. I don't know what happened next. I only remember Erich saying they won't soil German ground any longer and Hans-Georg replied with they are human beings like everyone and that Mr Rosenthal is one of the nicest neighbours he has ever had. Then there was a quarrel between you, Erich and Hans-Georg and suddenly I found myself in the automobile with a very angry Erich driving home. The whole trip he complained and swore: "They're going to see what will come of it, they should be careful!"

He wouldn't say anything, for my sake, but you overstepped the mark, interfering in political talk between men. That carried on the whole way home. I didn't dare to say something, Erich was so furious. When we were back at home he just put on his uniform and went to his comrades. When he came home later he had calmed down and didn't talk anymore about what had happened. Anyway, yesterday he started again. He said he won't visit you again and that he won't allow you to visit us in our flat. When he tried to forbid me writing letters to you we argued. He couldn't forbid that, I said. Then when Erich started shouting Marie woke up and cried. He calmed down and put her to bed. We didn't talk a word anymore and I cried until I fell asleep. In the morning at breakfast he said sorry and that I am allowed to write further letters but without political content, for you never know who will read them and maybe it is dangerous. When he went to work he kissed me goodbye. Everything is alright again but I am so sad. I will always write letters to you but how will we manage to meet again?

I'm so very sorry. Hugs.
A sad Eva

Letter from Lilli to Eva 3ʳᵈ March 1933

Dear Eva,

I'm very sorry about what happened but it probably had to be. Hans-Georg is also responsible for this. He could have simply ignored Erich's comment. Anyway, since the Reichstags fire the gangs of the SA have been unleashed; they had violently broken up an SPD election meeting on Saturday evening before you came. The justification was the danger of a Bolshevist conspiracy. Everyone had to prove their identity to make sure there was no wanted communist. If we hadn't had so much work to do in the shop, Hans-Georg would have been at the election meeting too. I'm so glad he wasn't there because then he would have been registered. The same Saturday evening a friend of Hans visited us to report what happened. And on Sunday you came. So it is understandable that he couldn't remain silent. And you know me, I say what I think.

I'm really sorry about how you have suffered because of this matter. Especially because I know how much you try to avoid any quarrels with Erich. I'm really happy and proud that you defended our friendship. It will be more difficult to visit each other, naturally, but I think I have a solution. Throughout the year I will take a few days holiday and go and visit your parents. Erich has to work then and I can see you and the children. I won't be able to come to birthdays or other celebrations but I will send presents for my godchild and Hildchen on their birthdays. I only hope Erich will recognise how dangerous his party for us all is. However, I don't believe in it. Hans-Georg and I are praying for the day after tomorrow. If Hitler hasn't intimidated everyone by then he hopefully won't get enough votes to remain chancellor of the Reich.

To write something about us: yesterday we did our first monthly account and just imagine, we earned more than Mr Schumacher in the last months! The first new thing we introduced, fresh and filled rolls every morning, went very well. Getting the bus to go and fetch the fresh rolls every morning before work was really worth it. Hans-Georg and I had the idea that if our shop continues to run like this that we will buy an automobile and then we can drive to the markets and fetch fresh products for our selection of goods. I hope all is well. Hugs,
Your Lilli

Letter from Eva to Lilli 17th March 1933
Dear Lilli,
I'm so happy about your shop running so well. I will keep my fingers crossed that it carries on in such a way. An automobile just for you, I can hardly imagine. In our village only the rich farmers like the Ranfts have one. Of course you are still welcome at my parent's house. Father does not really like Hitler very much. When Erich talked about your impossible and non-Aryan behaviour, father listened. But when he started to talk about the advantages and the coming election father became energetic. He said it is not appropriate to talk about such matters in the family circle. Honestly, I have seldom seen him that way. Erich went red but he held his mouth shut, even later. I think he respects father too much. Erich won't agree with you visiting my parents but he won't dare to set any rules for father and I know how to twist him around my little finger.
Concerning the election, farmer Ranft held a great celebration to honour Mr Hitler. He will now stay chancellor of the Reich, I think. However, although everybody spoke about the great success at the feast I think Erich was still discontented. He hardly talks to me about it. He only wants me to listen when he is enthusiastic or angry about

this matter. And when he heard the news he became really furious. He said: "How can there be so many blind people? That will change soon."

I wasn't at the election; I said I had to stay with the children. At first I thought Erich would disagree but then he confirmed my opinion. He has no time and we can't expect father and mother to take them at the moment. Besides, they had the little ones two days before the election during the last meeting of the comradeship. I don't think Erich was quite sure who I would vote for, for it is a secret voting. And he is right, I wouldn't have known either. However, enough of politics now.

I am so curious as to whether you will come to your next visit with a new automobile. The children are very well, they're flourishing. Mother is especially crazy about Hildchen. She says she is so attentive. She always looks at us and understands every word we say. I have to report just one thing; Mrs Salbei married. You know, the woman I worked with here in the shoe shop. At her age!? She is older than forty! Everyone in the village thought she would stay an old maid. They hadn't counted on the doggedness of Hein Kars, the farmhand of farmer Trost. He fell in love with her years ago when he was collecting some shoes for his dignitaries. Since then he regularly came to the shop as if by chance, even when I was still there, just to chat a bit. And every time he brought something for Mrs Salbei. A cauliflower, some potatoes. One time I saw that he had brought a bar of chocolate for her. When he was gone Mrs Salbei always said the same thing: "What is he hoping for?" And then she smiled. Now she seems to have understood. I am happy for them. Hein is really nice, always laughing and joking. Now perhaps even Mrs Salbei will smile more often. Father and mother were at the wedding ceremony in the church. Father said he only wants to see Hein wearing a suit once. You know what it's like here in the village.

47

Hope to see you again soon.
Your Eva

Letter from Lilli to Eva 27th June 1933

My dear Eva,

We finally did it. Hans-Georg and I bought an automobile. A second hand one. We removed the seats in the back of the car so that we have plenty room for our goods. Besides, there are only the two of us. Hans drives to the market regularly now and buys fresh products.

It is surprising how well the customers are accepting our changes. Our sales have improved once more. After much consideration I took another step yesterday; I gave Mr Burmeister my notice. In three weeks a new secretary will start working for him. A qualified secretary. Despite that, Mr Burmeister asked me to help her for one week so she can settle into the new job quickly. So there are four weeks left until I am independent. Isn't that funny? Independent - just like a man. Next week I am going to start my driving license so that I can drive to the market too. I know, in the village many people drive without a license but here in the city it is impossible. Nobody knows the village policeman with whom you can drink a beer in the evening. Especially as a woman they often stop you and control your papers. At first we wanted to start the whole thing more slowly but now with this success it has to be alright to do so. Everything is ok with me and Hans-Georg. But he is furious because they have forbidden the SPD. Two of his friends were arrested. I'm so glad that Hans isn't a member of the SPD. Sadly, our fears became reality. They spread fear and terror. I hope it won't get any worse. I also hope that Hans can control himself because more and more Braunhemden are coming to our shop. I'm sorry, I know Erich is one of them too but after what happened here I cannot call them anything other than that.

How are things in your family, is your mother recovering? Please give my regards to your parents.

Love,

Your Lilli

By the way, the chocolate is for you and the children and the cigars are for your father. Please ask him what he thinks about them. We are considering including them in our supply.

Letter from Eva to Lilli 10th October 1933

Dear Lilli,

It is unbelievable how fast your shop is developing. If it carries on like this you will become very rich and you will become a real lady. I'm really sorry about Hans-Georg's friends and it is wrong of course to forbid the SPD but not everything is bad. Erich told me that the party had to stop admitting new members because so many wanted to become part of the NSDAP. Could it be so wrong when so many people want to join? There was a great article in the newspaper about how much they do for children and the community. Erich urges me to join as well. He said it is not good for our reputation if I haven't got a party card. Farmer Ranft's son isn't a member either and they have already asked him why. It is only a question of time until they ask Erich as well. I just told him; as long as father is not a member then I won't join either. He was not really angry but only said: "You and your father."

I really love Erich but I'm glad to have father too. Mother's condition is not worse, that is simply sheer luck. She goes for a walk every evening with father. Often they walk to the Propheten lake and back.

Dear Lilli, many thanks for the chocolate. I haven't seen such a package before. It must have been shockingly expensive. I shared the chocolate with the children. Erich refused to take a piece. You know, because it is from you, even though he loves sweets so much and never refuses to eat anything made of sugar. Many thanks from

49

father also, the cigars are really marvellous. Have you got your
driving license already and will you come and visit me soon?
I miss you so much!
Hugs,
Your Eva

Diary entry 1st July 1945

Slowly but surely the bed linen is becoming scarce. I changed my
method and made nappies for Erich out of old pieces of cloth. I
refused to do it for a long time, it seemed so disgraceful but now
there is no other way. The old Mrs Bruns showed me how to fashion
great nappies from old cloth; she cared for her husband for two
years. He had to stay in bed for such a long time. She also suggested
that she can occasionally look in on Erich when I have to leave the
house. I will accept this offer even though I dislike it and I don't like
to leave Erich alone. Such an opportunity arose today. I couldn't
brush it aside. If everything goes well then we will have better times
soon. Because the refugees of farmer Ranft, who lived in his loft, will
move to the huts at the edge of the village, my opportunity came.
Everybody says that the refugees only cause problems. Not for me.
Their wives can no longer help Mrs Ranft, who is suffering from
rheumatism, so Heinz Ranft came to me. I was the first person he
thought of because Erich has been so reliable in the past. He needs
some help until other refugees arrive. And now I can help every
afternoon for a few hours. Should I have refused it? I accepted. We
haven't talked about the payment yet. Who would refuse to work at
a farm these days? I've got the feeling everything will turn out well
now.

Diary entry 2nd July 1945

Today, the doctor visited us again. He said Erich's condition hasn't changed, he has a high temperature and he is very weak. Nevertheless it seemed to me that he considers this to be good. I am going to the Ranft's this afternoon for the first time, I'm very excited. Today, of all days, Mrs Bruns has a visitor, her niece. Now Marie and Hildchen have to stay at home with their father. I hope so much that they won't have to change his nappies; even I have to force myself to do it. The smell is so vile that I have already had to vomit twice. Anyway, I don't want to think about it anymore, I'm looking forward to work. It is not only the chance of fine food; it is an opportunity to flee from all this, at least for a few hours. I feel bad when I think this way but I can ease my conscience with the thought that it is necessary for all of us. Especially the little ones need more food.

Letter from Eva to Lilli 20th January 1934

Dear Lilli,

Your last visit is already three weeks ago. It was such a lovely day. And it was so much fun to drive with your automobile through the countryside and to nibble on some chocolate. It was just like in the early days, only the two of us. I had nearly forgotten how free we once were. You haven't changed a bit; you stopped the car just to dance on a field. What luck that nobody saw us. That would have been great gossip for the village. Even father was enthusiastic about your new automobile. Later he named a few advantages of this kind of automobile. I didn't understand what he was talking about. I think he mentioned the induction pipe and the electric starter. It was a great event for Marie to sit on your lap driving around the yard. She spoke the whole evening of 'dwiwing da car'. Only Erich was angry again. He said it is far too dangerous to drive with a child on ones lap. Anyway, he couldn't spoil my good mood; it was such a nice day. Later, father teased Erich a bit. He asked him whether it isn't more dangerous to take a child with you on a tractor. Erich muttered: "That is something else." All the same, Erich seemed to have his mind on other things. And in the evening when we lay in bed he told me about it. Someone from the party is coming to Quickborn to organise the farming. Erich is worried about his organisation of the harvest because he is the head of the workers. I told him that Mr Ranft was always happy with his work. Sadly, this didn't calm him down. It is now important to stand the test of the party. He was really concerned and tossed and turned the whole night. I wasn't worried because my Erich is always honest and hard-working. And it was just how I thought it would be, the inspector, I call him inspector even though Erich told me he isn't one, he is a...I don't know. So, anyway, the inspector said that everything is running smoothly in Quickborn and he should go on like this for the Führer and the fatherland. I was really proud of Erich. Everything seems to be calming down. You can read in the newspaper that people are doing well under the regime of Hitler. There are nearly no unemployed people around. Last Sunday, the party organized a stew for the whole village. Everything was for free; they said it is for the community. There were speeches too. Farmer Ranft, who is now our mayor, was one of the speakers and some people from the party came from Hamburg. Honestly Lilli, step by step I can understand Erich now. Even father took part in the meeting. He said he mustn't like everything they do but their stew is nice. Nevertheless, I won't become a member of the party but I think it is very good that they are looking after the mothers. The chairman from Hamburg said there will be weekly meetings for the mothers soon so that the mothers can together devote themselves to the task of raising their children. Mayor Ranft also added that the party will provide the coffee and cake. Everybody clapped their hands and I did too.

I hope that all is well in Hamburg.

Love, Eva

Letter from Lilli to Eva 1st February 1934

Dear Eva,

I must say I'm very concerned. Now you are on their side too. After all I told you during my last visit; what the Braunhemden did to the Jewish shops in April in Berlin. They wanted to turn the people against the Jews. They don't shrink back from violence. Even here you constantly see more of them. Hans and I have got the feeling that they are everywhere. Even in the town offices when we need consignment notes for specialties from other countries, there are Braunhemden everywhere. They asked Hans twice whether it isn't un-German to buy products from France. Hans reacted very diplomatically; he said he has contracts which are binding. What should we do, we are dependent on their stamps.

Our shop is running better from month to month. All our changes are being accepted and we are getting more and more customers. We have a great number of regular customers buying the fresh products. But even the customers who come because of the specialties take something from the new supply nearly every time. It seems as if everybody has waited for us to arrive. Now the midday break is nearly over. Hans and I are going to the shop again.

Regards to your father and mother.

Love,

Lilli

Letter from Eva to Lilli 2nd March 1934

Dear Lilli,

I should also greet you from mother and father. All is well here. The children are growing and growing and can you believe that Erich had a wage increase from farmer Ranft again. It is well deserved, he works basically on his own on the farm. Since Mr Ranft became our mayor he's been spending nearly all his time in the office or is off to party meetings in Hamburg. One time he was even in Berlin. Just imagine, the Führer has shaken the hands of all delegates of the boroughs. He deserves it really, seeing as he now has so many problems with his son. He said in public that his father is blinded and that he cannot understand why he is following this Hitler. And he is not a child anymore, who does not know where he belongs; he is the same age as my Erich. The mayor was able to avoid worse things; he sent him to England to a special agricultural school. Thank goodness he can afford it. Yesterday, he said to Erich that it would be the best if he were to stay there forever and not only for two years. It is not a pleasant fate weighing down on Mr Ranft. Honestly said, I don't understand your concern. It is not bad to have everything in one hand. And the matter in Berlin? You told me that nearly no-one joined in. And after one day everything was over. Perhaps there were only a few of the party, certainly not all of them. You were not present and you know things are often exaggerated. There was not a word of it in the newspaper here.

Dear Lilli, I beg you not to talk badly about all Braunhemden. Erich is one of them and he is not a bad person. I hope you are well.

Love,

Eva

Letter from Lilli to Eva 20th March 1934

Dear Eva,

I'm sorry that I am replying so late but Hans-Georg and I had so much to do. It is unbelievable how well the shop is running. Hans had the idea to establish a delivery service for our wealthier clients. Not only for our products but also for the cold platters we now offer. They have been accepted so well that I now have a woman who helps several times during the week to prepare the ordered platters. Sadly, we now often have members of the NSDAP among our customers.

Hans has to pull himself together when he hears them talking and saying such thing as: "Everything for the well-being of the Führer!" He has now got the habit of carrying plates or covers during deliveries or when customers leave the shop so that it is not obvious that he does not respond to the Hitler salute. Hans would love to stop the deliveries for such persons but some of them have great influence and it would be very easy for them to cause problems for us.

Dear Eva, I'm sorry if you felt offended concerning Erich but I'm convinced that Hitler and his party have no good intentions. And I'm sure that the happenings in Berlin were planned by the party and that that was just the beginning. This year the first re-education camp has opened for political prisoners in Berlin. Mr Himmler personally inaugurated it and this was in the newspaper too. Up to now prisons and penitentiaries were sufficient. And you can imagine who goes into these re-education camps and with which methods the Braunhemden re-educate. I only think that if Hans had been a member of the SPD that he would have been imprisoned too. But thank goodness it hasn't happened and that we can concentrate on our shop.

I hope all is well.

Kind regards to your father and mother.

Lilli

Continuation Diary entry 2nd July 1945

It is ten o'clock in the evening. The children and Erich are already asleep. There is bed linen in the kitchen. I could already smell it as I closed the door. The children weren't lucky. I must show them how to rinse out the linen so that it doesn't smell so badly until the next laundry day. All my bones are aching, especially my knees. I had to scrub the tiling in the hall and in the kitchen for two hours. How big the hall is! It is bigger than our room and the kitchen together. After that I washed a whole washtub with laundry. I was able to wash in a heated washtub for the first time since the war ended. The Ranft family probably don't have to save their fuel for the winter. It is somewhat different doing such work for another family. Every time the old Mrs Ranft passed by me I had the feeling she was observing me and looking if I am working well enough. She gave me my orders but she did not talk to me any further. Earlier, at the evenings of the comradeship she sat together with us to knit and chat but today she seemed to have forgotten. It seems like she does not recognise me. A strange feeling. When her son came I felt better, he greeted me kindly. Today, he still didn't talk about the payment but when I wanted to go home a parcel lay on my jacket with "For Eva" on it. It is like Christmas, in the parcel I found a pound of flour, potatoes for a whole meal and also a piece of ham and a small strip of bacon. I'm a bit ashamed because I cut a little piece off and ate it with a slice of bread. How long it has been since I have eaten such a delicacy. And still the taste is so familiar. Tomorrow, I have to be there at two o'clock; Mrs Ranft wants the windows to be cleaned whilst there is daylight. I'm a bit concerned about how long it will take to clean all the windows of this huge house. Erich is groaning now. I hope he will have a calm night.

Letter from Eva to Lilli 5th January 1935

Dear Lilli,

Many thanks for your Christmas parcel; the children were so happy about the sweets. I gave the wine to father because without Erich I don't want to drink wine. Father took it with pleasure. He said that we don't know what we're missing. He sends his greetings. I hope you are well and that you had a nice start into the New Year.

Love,

Eva

Letter from Eva to Lilli 20th December 1936

Dear Lilli,

Many thanks for the parcel but I must beg you not to write any further and not to send parcels. Erich said he won't be able to keep your comments concerning the party to himself anymore. I really don't understand you. Everybody is still well and you are better off from year to year. It is not necessary to always find something to criticise.

All the best for your future life,

Eva

Letter from Eva's father to Lilli 27th March 1937

Dear Lilli,

Sadly I have to tell you that my beloved wife passed away on 25th March after much suffering. It seems to sound harsh but maybe it was a blessing for her. I think it is a shame that two friends separate because of Mr Hitler and that I must be the one to inform you about this sad event in such a way.

In deep mourning,

Karl Lohmann

Letter from Lilli to Eva's father 28th March 1937

Dear Mr Lohmann,

I want to express my deep condolences to you. I will always remember the hospitality and the nice manner of your wife. I'm grateful for having known her. I hope you will recover from this loss. I think your daughters and grandchildren will be a great consolation. I regret the break up between Eva and myself very much also. I learned from your letter that you aren't an ardent admirer of Hitler and his followers either. I always tried to make Eva understand with which methods

these gentlemen work and what their true views are. I assume that she couldn't bear the conflict of my words and the things her husband wants in the long run. I hope Eva and I will find a way in the future.
Yours   sincerely,
Elisabeth Marten

Letter from Eva's father to Lilli 4th April 1937

Dear Lilli,
Many thanks for your compassionate words. I hope for a better future for your friendship too. Thank you so much for the enclosed cigars. They had a wonderful flavour.
Kind   regards,
Karl Lohmann

Letter from Hans-Georg to Eva 3rd January 1938

Dear Eva,
It is surely a surprise for you that I am writing to you. But sadly the news I want to tell you are such that I cannot keep them back. Lilli had a serious accident two weeks ago. A lorry hit her bike and she was thrown against the wall of a house. One of her legs was broken and her face had abrasions. This wouldn't be that bad but Lilli was pregnant in the fifth month. You surely know that we concentrated on the shop and we didn't want to have children for the time being. After Lilli knew about the pregnancy she utterly changed. She was so happy. Even I was very glad. Therefore, we bought the flat above our shop so Lilli could carry on working. That was very important for her. What inspired her most was the prospect of contacting you again, for she always said that when women can talk about children that everything else is unimportant. Now everything has changed. Lilli lost her child at the scene of the accident. The doctor said that her injuries are not so serious as to require her to stay in bed and that she should

have gotten up a week ago. Nevertheless, she refuses to do so, she looks around and when I want to talk to her she always says: "Not now Hans, I'm not feeling well."

The nurse told me her soul is injured. I am at a loss as to what to do so I am writing to you. Of course I know about your rift but I know how important you always were for Lilli. So I ask you now to be at our side in this time of trouble. Please write her a few comforting words. With this request for help I greet you and your family,

Hans-Georg Marten

Letter from Eva to Lilli 6th January 1938

Dear Lilli,

I heard about your accident. I was deeply shocked. I cannot express how sorry I am for your loss. However, I'm at the same time infinitely glad that I haven't lost you through this accident. I don't think I have ever regretted something more in my life than my last letter to you. I was very annoyed at that time, especially because for all of us everything was going so well. I couldn't see anything bad. I wanted to enjoy this lovely time undisturbed. But since then there has been no day that I haven't thought of you. Every now and then I started writing letters just to crumple them up and throw them into the fire. But when my beloved mother died I had written a letter but fate didn't want me to send it away. I had already reached the Bahnhofs road and was on my way to the post office when I met Erich. He wanted to go to the post office too, to fetch a parcel for the Ranft family. He asked me what I wanted there, of course. I paused shortly; I nearly lied to him at that time. But then I told him the truth. And then he talked me out of it. I simply didn't dare to argue with my husband on the street. Erich wouldn't have understood it. Now I have told him that you are a part of my life and that I won't give you up for his party. I'm still no member of the party. Like father. Erich was really

59

angry; he went to the headquarters in the evening. He calls the office the headquarters. He returned late. I heard him but I didn't get up. In the morning he pretended nothing was wrong. I hope you aren't annoyed anymore and that you write back to me. Please give me the address of the hospital. The connection to Hamburg has really improved and I would love to visit you. Father has already said he would look after the children. There is news also: I had twins. They are one year old. You see, there is much to do for you as an aunt. Of course, it would be even nicer to visit you at your new flat. I'm very curious to see how large it is.

Kind regards from father and I should send you his get-well-soon wishes. I should also greet you from Marie. She cannot remember you but can remember your presents. For her you are aunt 'Chocolate'. Please write to me and recover quickly. You have a job as a godmother to do here.

Dear Lilli, I miss you so much.

Yours Eva

Letter from Lilli to Eva 9th January 1938

Dear Eva,

Thank you so much for your letter. I cannot tell you how glad I was when I received it. It was like awaking from a bad dream for me. Sadly, this dream was reality. After I read the letter I cried for an hour. Poor Hans didn't know how to comfort me. I cried and even screamed. I couldn't stand the injustice which I noticed in this moment. After one hour I got a terrible headache but I didn't care. Since then I have been able to think about other things, not only the accident. Especially you and Hans-Georg, of course, who had a really heavy burden with me. The bottom line is that he lost his child too. Meanwhile, I've been getting up and the doctor said I can return home in two days if I take good care of myself. So, if you like you can visit me at home. Hans organised the painting jobs and the move. When I go home everything will be ready. Now I'm looking forward to it a little bit.

Please greet your father and tell Marie that aunt 'chocolate' will send her chocolate as soon as she is at home.

Hugs,

Lilli

Letter from Eva to Lilli 1ˢᵗ February 1938

Dear Lilli,

It was such a nice visit at your home. How impressive and large your flat is. Four rooms and a real toilet with a cistern. What was really amazing was the bathtub. A tub not out of zinc but covered with enamel and above it a heater for the hot water. No tiresome dragging of jugs full with hot water. I would love to have one, for Erich takes a bath daily. Marie couldn't believe it when you put her into the bathtub immediately. She told Erich every detail about it when we returned; about the room which is only for the bath tub and where she could decide how hot the water was. She told him that aunt Lilli (now she talks of aunt Lilli) just had to turn the little wheel and the water was warm. I saw it exactly in Erich's eyes; he would love to have such a bathtub too. Anyway, after Marie was in bed, he talked badly about it. If everyone wanted such a bath the community wouldn't be able to afford it. However, I didn't listen.

Dear Lilli, I'm so glad about your recovery and about us, naturally. I must tell you that Hans-Georg surprised me. How he cooked and afterwards when we drank a cup of coffee he cleaned the dishes. I couldn't expect that from Erich, for him this is a woman's job.

You know, there is something new. Father has a girlfriend!

It is not really serious but they meet every afternoon for a coffee. She is the widow of the old blacksmith Trapp. I'm happy for my father.

Erich said it is not a done thing, one year after mother's death and at his age. And I was naughty; I said to Erich that he should tell father personally so that he doesn't make a mistake. I, as his daughter, couldn't talk with him, that just isn't done. Erich hummed and hawed, he thought about it and said: "It's not really that bad." I won't talk about it anymore, I don't dare but I like to tease Erich a bit sometimes.

Marie and Hildchen greet you kindly and please send my regards to Hans-Georg.

I hope you are well.

Hugs,

Eva

Letter from Lilli to Eva 21st February 1938

Dear Lilli,

I feel better now after having gone through a low last week. I have already told you that I had to go to the hospital for a last examination. That was last week. Hans-Georg shut the shop without further ado, because our temporary help does the household for her ill mother on that day, to accompany me. He is a real sweetheart. It was a good idea because after the examination the doctor looked at me strangely. When I sat together with Hans in his room he came out with it. "Dear Mrs Marten," he said, "you will never be able to have children."

He explained why but I didn't listen. Hans took me home. I felt exactly the way I did when I lost the child. Without hope. Everything seemed so senseless. In the evening I pulled myself together. I couldn't leave Hans alone again. I thought of you, Marie, Hildchen and the little ones and I decided to spoil your children from now on, if you will agree. I'm still sad and there are moments when I have to be very strong. In such moments I look for a job which occupies me. When I cannot put away new products, I rearrange the stock or clean the shop window. You know how big it is. Hans does not say anything even if I rearranged the stock and cleaned the window last week. He knows me so well; I'm often surprised about it.

At the moment I am thinking about something else. Hans-Georg wants to buy a car just for me. He does not want me to use the bike anymore after all this and also because of the increasing traffic in the city. A car just for me, only for my shopping. I don't know, isn't it mad?

Oops, I nearly forgot the time, the midday break is over. I have to go to the shop. Hans is visiting a customer to talk about the delivery of platters and specialties for a big celebration.

Greet the children! The enclosed sweets are for them to share. The pralines are just for you. The cigars are for your father, of course.

Hugs,

Lilli

Diary entry 3rd July 1945

How am I meant to endure this? Erich vomited the whole night. I haven't slept a minute and even the children couldn't sleep. They're staying at home today. We've managed to wash all the laundry today. We are lucky, there is no rain today and it is windy so everything will be dry by the evening. But it cannot go on like this. The children need to sleep. I will put Erich's bed into the kitchen and the table and the chairs in our room when I return from the Ranfts' today. I haven't liked the idea up until now because I don't want to have the smell in the kitchen but it is everywhere now anyway and maybe the children will be able to sleep without disturbance. The doctor has not been here for many days but during his last visit he said he couldn't do anything more. "Now your husband has to make it on his own", he said.

All the abscesses are open now and are less scabby. Thanks to the chamomile baths they haven't become inflamed. Nevertheless, Erich is in a kind of permanent sleep. Sometimes he opens his eyes for a short moment but I don't think he recognises us. He often fantasises but you can hardly understand what he says. Just now and then I notice a name. He still does not notice it when he has to relieve himself, he is like a grown-up newborn. When I give him soup or mush he eats everything eagerly without knowing what he is doing. Mrs Scheeßel, our neighbour, says I should be happy, many were taken prisoner and if my husband hadn't deserted the army then he wouldn't be here. I noticed her underlying accusation. May God forgive me, I prayed so hard for his return but sometimes I'm really in despair. I tell the children the complete opposite: How lucky we are that their father is back and that everything will be alright. If only I could believe it.

Diary entry 16th July 1945

Erich has now been home for three weeks and today he opened his eyes for the very first time and he recognised me. There was a smile on his face and he squeezed my hand for a moment. I don't know what to think, the last weeks were so exhausting. Not one night without changing the bed linen at least once. And even if I like going to the Ranft's house, the work is pretty hard. When there is nothing to do in the house, the old Mrs Ranft sends me to clean out the stables, onto the field or into the vegetable garden. Mr Ranft is very generous but sadly he is only present for a very short time before I go to say hello and to put a parcel with groceries onto my jacket. Without this food Erich wouldn't have recovered. When I look at him I think I can sometimes see that he has gained weight in his face. Even his ribs aren't prodding out anymore. For the first time I truly believe in Erich's recovery.

Letter from Eva to Lilli 15th March 1938

Dear Lilli,

Thank you for your parcel. The children were so happy and Marie asked when we will be going to aunt Lilli's house to take a bath again. Imagine, I caught Erich nibbling my pralines. At first I was surprised and suspected the children when I noticed that one praline was gone but they said they were innocent. So I thought I was wrong. It didn't come into my mind that Erich could have stolen the praline. But as Erich was on his way to the toilet I heard a rustle in the hall and when I got up I saw Erich eating one of my pralines. I coughed. He jumped. He nearly spat out the nice praline. And you know what he said? "These are very fine pralines", and that he had asked himself if we can afford them. When I answered that the pralines are from you, he just said: "I thought they were gone long ago" and went to bed without a further word. Isn't that funny?

Can you believe that I am alone at home for four days? Erich is in Austria. At first there was a great celebration at farmer Ranft's after we managed to take Austria back into our possession. And during the celebration Mr Ranft said: "We have to go there!"

I think he had drunk a bit too much but the next morning he fetched Erich. They went to Hamburg by car and then to Wien by train. Erich is having a proper holiday for four whole days and Mr Ranft is paying for everything. Erich is very hard-working, he deserves it.

Tomorrow, he returns; I'm curious about what he will tell me.

It seems to be serious between father and Mrs Trapp. Imagine, a few days ago I saw her coming out of father's door when I had to get up early. They should announce it officially otherwise there will be gossip.

Dear Lilli, I'm so sorry about what the doctor told you. You are so courageous. But who knows, sometimes even the doctors are wrong and until then you can pamper your godchild. By the way, a few days ago Hildchen came to me and asked why she hasn't got an aunt 'chocolate' too. The big one always stresses that the chocolate is from her aunt. I always say then "as sisters you have to share everything and so it is enough to have one godmother". This calms Hildchen down.

What I cannot understand is how you can think about whether you want an automobile or not. I would take one immediately. Let Hans be good to you, he loves to do it and you deserve it. I must greet you kindly from father. It is actually a little embarrassing for him but he takes the cigars willingly because he has known you for such a long time.

A big kiss from the children. Marie has painted the enclosed picture. It is supposed to be a dog, she probably hopes that you will give her one. Even if I tell her again and again that we have no room for a dog. "But there are small dogs too", she always says then. Honestly, actually I wouldn't mind but for Erich a dog must be large and he would never keep him in the house.

I wish you a wonderful summer. Maybe you can manage to visit us soon with the new automobile?

Hugs,
Your Eva

Letter from Lilli to Eva 17th November 1938

Dear Eva,

I'm sorry about how long I haven't written to you. There was so much work to do. As well as working in the shop I also worked for half a year for Mr Burmeister again. He was in real trouble because his secretary was suddenly ill and couldn't work anymore. At the moment it is very difficult to find a substitute so he asked me for help. He raised my former wage by nearly half. Hans-Georg and I were able to use the money to pay for the flat we bought and I couldn't talk him out of the car for me. But now I'm happy that I have a successor so I can find the time to write to you. I was so glad about the picture of Marie. I took it to be framed straight away. And how? With my new car. It is baby-blue, a small DKW. You were right; why should I do without it? And it is so much fun to drive with this small car. You can get everywhere. It is much easier to drive than the big one. Anyway, I had the picture framed and now it is hanging in the shop on the wall directly next to the cash register. Many people have spoken to me about it and nearly all of them recognised that it is a dog. We are now thinking about whether we should buy a little dog, maybe a poodle. During the business hours he could stay in the private area and in the yard. I won't be alone then when Hans delivers platters or fetches new products. Hans-Georg isn't convinced yet but when I beg him he will surely change his mind. However, sometimes I wonder how can I think about such things when there is violence breaking out everywhere? They destroyed Jewish shops everywhere in Hamburg and the SS has taken Jews out of their houses and brought them away. Even our neighbour, Mr Rosenthal. You remember the reason for the first quarrel between Erich and Hans-Georg. They even led him away. His wife said he will be taken to a camp, that's what the SS-men mentioned and they laughed and said: "Now you will meet people like yourself."

This is so terrible. Mrs Rosenthal could only escape because her husband called her Mrs Schmidt and said she should close the shop now. Hans gave the poor woman the advice to go abroad and he offered her some money. We don't know whether she has gone but since then we haven't seen her and her children. Everything is normal now; only Mr Rosenthal's shop burnt down. Hans and I are thinking seriously about selling our shop and going abroad too. Hans has a distant relative in England. She says she has plenty of space and for the interim we could live there. We won't be penniless. But it would be so hard to leave Hamburg, the shop, my mother and especially you and the children behind.

Dear Eva, I will visit you soon. The parcel is the same as always. Pralines for you, cigars for your father and chocolate for the children. A kind hug,

Your Lilli

Letter from Eva to Lilli 16th December 1938

Dear Lilli,

You frightened me with your last letter. Now that we are together again I couldn't imagine losing you to England. Concerning the bad events, such things haven't happened here. Honestly said, I don't know whether there are Jews around or not. I read reports about the murder of this vom Rath but you couldn't sense anything here. Erich complains about the Jews, of course, but he's been doing this since he became a member of the party. At the same time he does not even know one of them I think. What frightens me more is when Erich talks about Czechoslovakia. He said we won't let our brothers in Czechoslovakia down and if we don't receive the area voluntarily then the Führer will use force. After all, we are important again. I don't know if we are right but I hope so much that there won't be a war, even when Erich says we are so strong again. Wasn't it the same in the last war? Father told us how the emperor declared war on everybody because he felt so strong. And how much he believed in it until he was wounded. However, you know father's stories about the war. At any rate, I don't want to see my Erich go to war. He would be one of the first who would volunteer. Who knows whether he would be lucky like father or rather have the same fate as your father.

Dear Lilli, I beg you, stay here, what shall I do without you? And back then, in the shop, you always told me it won't become that bad. I hope everything stays the same for the children. We have such a wonderful life. And not everybody has as much luck. Father told me yesterday that Anna, my little sister, told him her husband often drinks too much. One time he hit her when she wanted to talk about it. Can you imagine that? Rainer, the nice Rainer, how friendly he always was. And he is a civil servant. I could hardly believe it. I only hope there won't be gossip, otherwise the children in the street will notice. I don't want that in any case. I'm sorry for Anna, of course, I will visit her in the next couple of days and maybe I can help her somehow.

Dear Lilli, I mustn't forget to thank you for your generous parcel. You spoil not only the children but even father and me. He thanks you also. The pralines you sent were even more delicious than the ones before. And you won't believe it! Erich did it again. I always counted the pralines and every second day there was one missing. He is more cautious now but he couldn't stop himself. I couldn't keep from teasing him, of course. I told him we have a problem; our children steal and then lie about it. You can imagine how he reacted: "That is unbelievable; we have to take drastic action."

Only afterwards he asked me what the children had stolen. Then I told him about the missing pralines. "There is no other answer than the children. Nobody was in the flat and you would never take one of Lilli's pralines voluntarily", I said to him and asked him what kind of hard punishment he suggests. He went red then; I saw it even with the low light of the night lamp. He said it is not that bad, he also did such things when his mother was still alive. Children have to be mischievous, otherwise they wouldn't be real children and we shouldn't talk about it with them but rather leave them their secret. After that he was really breathless. Of course I agreed but I knew and he knew that I knew. I think I slept with a smile on my face that night. The children send their love and Marie said that you should tell your husband to hug you in her place. Isn't that sweet?

Dear Lilli, I miss you much, maybe business in the shop will allow for a visit soon.
Hugs,
Your Eva

Diary entry 20th June 1945

This morning the miracle happened. Erich was clear and spoke. Directly after the children got up he awoke and called me. We were sitting in our room at the table. It was nearly as if someone had taken our breath away. Not one of us dared to make a noise because who knows, maybe it was just another illusion. When the calling was repeated with emphasis the girls started to talk in confusion. It was very difficult to calm them down and stop them from going into the kitchen immediately. At first I went on my own and it was really unbelievable. He hugged me and said: "Eva, I'm back."

I don't like to write it but the hug was so strange. I loosened the embrace at once. Luckily I had an excuse. "There are some people who want to see you and talk to you."

It was as if he had forgotten them. "The children, of course, the children."

At first I let the big ones go to him. Everything was fine until the moment Marie couldn't hold back her tears. How gruff his voice became: "There is nothing to cry about, I'm home again", he shouted. The children were very shocked. I took them out of the room then. I didn't like to let the little ones go to him but he insisted. So I let them go and it went really well. The little ones seem to make him happy. I did not leave them there for long; I noticed that talking was still very exhausting for him. Now he is asleep, what luck that today is Sunday. I hope the big ones will have another conversation with him today which won't end like the first, otherwise I don't know how I can leave them alone with him tomorrow.

Letter from Lilli to Eva 21st December 1938

Dear Eva,

For now you mustn't be worried. Hans and I aren't ready to leave Germany yet. Such things have to be prepared carefully and do not happen from one day to another. Nevertheless, Hans-Georg has planned to visit his cousin at the beginning of next year for one week. He wants to look for possibilities for us to find another income. Hans speaks English very well. I am taking lessons in the evening from a teacher who lived in England for three years before the last war. She says in the part of Cornwall were she had lived there was only farming. But this is more than twenty years ago and Hans's cousin lives far in the north, on the east-coast of York. However, as I said, it is just one possibility to flee from these people. Because of the Sudeten German there won't be a war anymore. Hitler got the area he wanted. I only hope that he is satisfied now and that he will keep the promises he gave in Munich.

Dear Eva, when I read your words about Anna and her husband I was really furious. Why can a man just hit his wife? Is it enough that he is stronger? I really hope that you and your father gave Anna the advice to leave her husband. If you ask me, a man who hits his wife once will do it again. What luck that your sister hasn't had children with this man. Talk to Erich. Isn't it in his eyes un-German to hit a woman? Can't an Aryan man make it clear to this other man how to treat a woman properly?

What about your nice father? What about his romance? Is he courting already? Honestly said, I don't believe in it but I don't think it is bad if he is happy. Let the people talk. I think it is a bit similar in our shop. Always at the same time the same customers meet in our shop. Mostly women, of course. It is as if they have arranged this

71

meeting even if one of them always shouts: "You here? What a coincidence!"

My point is that it is like in a small village. There is always a topic which is of current interest. For a time it was the expulsion of our Jewish neighbour, then it was the love-affair of our district pastor with a post office clerk and now it is the journey around the world of one of these ladies, who regularly sends postcards to one of them from different places in the world. But what I surely learnt from this is that when there are no changes or new stories concerning an affair the ladies switch to another story. I think this will happen in your father's case. At first everyone will be indignant but after a while it won't be interesting anymore.

I hope you and the children are well, give them a hug from me. I won't be able to visit you in the near future but we will certainly see each other in the new year. The parcel is the same as always.

Hugs,

Your Lilli

Letter from Eva to Lilli 23rd December 1938

Dear Lilli,

It is very comforting for me to hear about your plans not to leave Germany so very soon. Meanwhile, I am not worrying about a war anymore, for Erich is talking more about the success of the Führer and less about a war. He has been saying for three months that England and France have submitted to the will of the Führer in Munich. Maybe we were right then?

Still there is father and he worries us. He won't listen to me. I used all my powers of persuasion but he is really stubborn. He neither wants to marry Mrs Trapp, nor will he agree to reduce their meetings. He says they both are grown-ups and the whole thing is not my business. I pointed out the reputation of our family, naturally. Imagine what he

72

answered: "Love cannot be wrong and if people want to talk, let them talk!"

Sadly, it is not like in your shop here; in our village they will never forget such things. Someday, father will be the mad guy who has a lover despite his age. And you know, I think even this would not matter to him. He really worries me. But there is good news from Anna. I told you about Anna and her husband in my last letter. I'm sorry that you got so angry about it because it is over and done with. I talked to Anna and she told me that Rainer apologised with a bunch of flowers.

After that they talked it over and Rainer promised he wouldn't drink so much anymore if Anna would stop worrying about just one beer. Anna is happy again now and the striking wasn't as bad as it at first seemed to be. Anna told me personally that it just was a light tap and that Rainer didn't mean to be so angry. I have the feeling that everything, apart from father, is getting better.

The children are very well. They were very enthusiastic about the new sweets with the sticky cherry filling. Even I tasted them and found them delicious. Erich still takes one of my pralines regularly; it seems as if he is glad to be able to blame the children. He takes at least one daily. The ones with the golden wrapping filled with alcohol are always first. I thought about whether I should ask him if he isn't worried about our children drinking alcohol. But I didn't, for honestly speaking, I'm happy when he eats pralines from you and I don't want to spoil the fun he has. Father thanks you again. The children say they love you. They are so excited because of Christmas. Farmer Ranft took the photograph of the children, which I have enclosed, with his camera at a celebration for children. All families who have at least one person in the party got two photographs two weeks later via post. You can simply cut off the imprint of the NSDAP Quickborn on the paper.

I wish you and Hans-Georg a very merry Christmas. I'm looking
forward to seeing you in the next year.
With love,
Your Eva

Diary entry 21st July 1945

Everything is alright. I just came home and Marie and Hildchen
reported to me that their father slept nearly the whole time. He only
called Marie once for some water. It seems as if he used the empty
milk bottle for the first time for his urine. It is standing half-full
beside his bed. I had put it on the chest which I use as a bedside
locker. I didn't say anything but he understood anyway. It will still
take a long time until he is able to go downstairs and go to the toilet
in the yard. However, this is a beginning. I don't know when he will
be able to use the bucket but I hope soon. My supply of old cloth is
nearly empty and the used ones are not in good shape anymore
because of the washing. The little ones were already asleep when I
came home and I sent the big ones to bed immediately. Today, I
wasn't able to leave the Ranft's farm until very late. Mr Ranft had to
go to Hamburg because of the harvest results and the old farmer's
wife didn't let me go. Each time I finished one job she gave me
another. Now I've opened the parcel she gave me, it is very meagre.
A few potatoes, which are not enough for a meal, and a piece of old
bread. Nothing more. I'm glad that her son will prepare the parcel
tomorrow. I'm so tired but I just had to sit for a while to think a bit.
I hope for a quiet night.

Diary entry 22nd June 1945

I wasn't able to sleep at all tonight. Erich called me just as I had
gone to bed. He wanted to use the bucket, finally. But sadly, he is
weaker than I thought; we managed to make him sit on the bucket

but he couldn't keep his balance and fell together with the bucket onto the floor. Thank god he hasn't injured himself, for the edges of the bucket are quite sharp. To get him back into bed again was not so difficult because he is still very light. But his impatience was testing. Erich was angry. He asked me whether I have nothing better for him. At first nothing came to my mind but then I had the right idea. I fetched the mother's old saucepan, which I had hidden in the loft during the war for fear of the metal collectors. How scary it is up there at night. But it was worth it. Erich was satisfied and the saucepan is solid enough. The cleaning is a bit difficult because the pot is so large and heavy but if I can avoid the nappies I'm very grateful. Now he is asleep, the children are in school and I can enjoy a quiet moment to myself.

Letter from Lilli to Eva 20th March 1939

Dear Eva,

How happy I was to receive the photograph of your two angels. You can imagine what I did. On the same day I drove to our photographer and had a frame made. Yesterday I was able to fetch it. Now the two of them are hanging above the picture that Marie drew. Two customers have already asked me whether one of them is the artist. It is wonderful to have you all in my life and that makes it all the more difficult to write these lines. Hitler did it again; he founded the Protectorate Bohemia and Moravia on foreign soil and believe me, dear Eva, there is no justification for that. Hans and I don't believe that he will ever be satisfied. And even England does not believe it anymore. Hans-Georg reads English newspapers regularly, which he gets from our English supplier, and he says they are preparing their people for a war. Nobody believes Hitler and his followers when they make promises and talk about peace anymore. Therefore we have decided: Hans and I will go to England.

This morning I accompanied Hans to the airport. I think he must have arrived at his cousins already. Now that we have made up our mind it all seems to be happening faster than I thought. The day before yesterday one of our suppliers, who owns a grocery shop in Altona, was here. He was very interested when we told him that we want to sell our shop and after he saw our accounts and returns he was very enthusiastic. Next week he will talk to his bank manager and if he hasn't got any objections then he will make us an offer. I can hardly believe it; if everything is alright then we will be leaving Germany this year. We wanted to take mother with us but she refused: "You cannot move an old tree without it dying," she said. I can understand that, of course. You know, I would love to take you and the children with me. If only that were possible. But we aren't that far away and who knows, when the situation has calmed down and Hitler isn't in power anymore we may come back again. In any case I will definitely visit you before we go. I want to say goodbye to your father personally, of course. I hope he is well. The parcel is the same as always. Hugs for the little ones.
Yours sincerely,
Lilli

Letter from Eva to Lilli 25th May 1939
Dearest Lilli,
You actually want to leave Germany. Dear Lilli, it is very difficult for me to believe it although I can understand you. Erich has been all excited since the foundation of the protectorate, he talks about nothing else. "Nobody can beat the Führer, he will show everyone. And the English should be careful; there is no war we couldn't win with him as Führer."
Should there be a war I am happy, of course, that you are safe. I worry a lot about Erich; it seems as if he is just waiting to take part in the

war. I asked him whether he had never heard father's stories. But he just wouldn't listen to me and said that they hadn't got a Führer at that time and asked me if I can't see what the Führer has already done for the people. I didn't say anything more, for otherwise it would have started a quarrel. Father says he can understand you very well and if he were younger then he would accompany you. It is so strange; in the newspaper and all around me everybody is in a good mood, everyone acclaims the Führer like Erich and they don't fear a war. Father and you seem to be an exception. It is like you have lost your mind or all the others have. The strange thing is that I believe that it is all the others who no longer know what is right or wrong. But what can I do? I cannot go. I have to go on living here. I have to think about the children and Erich, of course. So I hope you are wrong and that everything turns out to be ok. I'm happy every day that I've got the children and I try to just live my life. And there are enough things which worry me.

Father succeeded: The whole village is talking about him and his girlfriend. Mrs Barns from the bakery approached me and said how difficult it must be with my father. At first I wanted to give her a piece of my mind but then I thought about what you told me and just nodded my head in a resigned way. Perhaps it is really better not to give them more things to talk about. Sadly, I also have bad news. The day before yesterday I saw Rainer coming out of the pub and he was staggering. I didn't tell Anna. I feel sorry for the poor girl.

The children are wonderful; they are growing day by day and are never disobedient. Only Hildchen is different. She often asks when I forbid something, why she isn't allowed to do it. Marie never asks. Sometimes it seems to me like Marie is the younger girl, even though she is much taller than Hilde. Both greet you, of course. And father sends his thanks again for the marvellous cigars. You are so generous, really.

Hugs,
Your Eva

Letter from Lilli to Eva 30th May 1939

Dear Eva,

I have already told you about Hans-Georg's journey to England. He has now returned and is safe and sound. What he reported was sobering. York is far smaller than Hamburg and very rural. A shop like ours is not possible there. Hans has travelled a lot during the week. He says that we could earn money by selling agricultural equipment. He also said that what he saw being sold in the businesses over there is not nearly as advanced as what we have in Germany. With the right connections we may manage to do something there. But this would only be possible without a war. But we fear a war and that is why we want to go to England! And so Hans tested another possibility. He said there are many small farms which hardly make enough money for the owners to survive on. If we were to buy some of them and put them together it would be possible to be cheaper than the small ones. And even the use of larger agricultural machines would be worthwhile. Hans said the farmers there do everything with their own hands. But honestly, can you imagine me as a farmer's wife? Milking in the morning and mucking out in the evening. I really don't know whether I can do that. Hans thinks that when we are finally there that we would have the possibility to move to a big city, maybe London. There are far better opportunities to start a shop in a city. It's going to be a while until then. The supplier's bank is willing to help him but before they commit to anything they want to check our accounts and the director wants to visit our shop personally. Our supplier said the bank will be in touch with us within the next four weeks. Now two weeks have passed and we still haven't heard anything. I think we should ask but Hans said that that would give the impression that we need to sell urgently and that they would then try to bring down the price. You know my impatience, for me it is agonizing to wait. Sometimes I just want to shout in Hans-Georg's face when he is so relaxed. But I know, of course, that he has much more experience in such matters and that it would be unfair to blame him.

Meanwhile, I've been occupied with the preparations. How much luggage should we take with us, should we put our furniture into storage or should we sell everything? Taking it with us would be too expensive and there wouldn't be enough space at cousin May's anyway.

Is it okay with you if I visit at the beginning of August? Maybe 5th August; it is a Saturday. By then I'll have everything important for our trip prepared. I only hope that we sell the shop, imagine if the buyer or the bank say no.

Dear Eva, what you have written about the enthusiasm for Hitler among the people is not quite the same here in Hamburg. In the shop we often hear people whisper: "He wouldn't start a war, would he?" Often it is the wives of the wealthier people who say that. Perhaps there are some people in your village who disagree with these politics, but who really dares to say such things in public? I only hope for you and the children that everyone and especially Erich see how wrong this is. I didn't want to go any further into it in my last letter but I didn't believe in Rainer's change of character. You know my attitude towards violent men. She has to leave this man at all costs.

Just think, yesterday we received the order to present a certificate which proves that we are Aryan. I also know of some customers who also needed to present this certificate, but their husbands were candidates for the party. I assume someone dislikes us. Now we have to sort all this out as well. You can imagine how I'm not looking forwardto this. I don't want to have any trouble before our journey. I hear a

lorry coming into the yard, we are receiving new products.
Hugs for the little ones and greet your father from me.
Love,
Lilli

Diary entry 26th July 1945

Today, Erich demanded to sleep in our room again. I tried to make clear how embarrassing it is for the girls when I have to lift him onto the pot but he insisted. He seems to have no sense of shame anymore. This evening, when I return from the Ranft's we will do it. We are going to put Erich on a chair, I will hold him and the girls will carry the bed into our room. I don't know whether Erich will manage to walk from the kitchen to the bed. I hope we don't need to carry him. How I'm always ashamed to write such things. But everything has changed. Today, as I bent over him to take the full bottle of urine from the chest of drawers he caressed my cheek for the first time. I jumped; I nearly dropped the bottle. I told him that I've been so nervous since the planes from Hamburg having been flying over and dropping the remainders of the bombs. It was a lie; he disgusts me with his raw hands. I know it is wrong. He still is my husband.

How much I loved it back then when he caressed my cheeks. His hands were warm and soft then and he always took good care of his hands although he had to work hard.

In ten minutes it is three o'clock and the children will be coming from school. At four o'clock I have to be at the Ranft's. I don't know how I would stand it all without the hours on the farm.

Letter from Eva to Lilli 13th August 1939

Dear Lilli,
It is terrible; tonight, there was suddenly a knock at our door. Erich

thought it was a mission and immediately jumped out of the bed. I wasn't allowed to go to the door, that wouldn't be proper when he is on duty. You always have to be on duty for the people and for the Führer. How quickly he put on his uniform and opened the door. You can imagine how surprised I was when he came back, with the words "for you", as fast as he had gone. It was Anna; she sat with a raincoat over her nightie in our living room. When I switched on the light I saw the horror. Her whole face was swollen and she couldn't open her right eye. I didn't say anything; I simply took her into my arms. She cried like in the early days when she used to come into my bed because she had had a bad dream. Sadly this was no dream. She had opened a letter from the town offices, in which Rainer was threatened with losing his job if he doesn't go to his shift once more and doesn't have a good excuse or if he starts his shift under the influence of alcohol again. When Rainer came home she spoke to him about it. Rainer left without one word. But when he came back later he insulted her and asked her how she dare open his letters. And then he hit her. Anna said she stumbled and fell against the edge of a chair. Rainer just turned away and went to bed. Isn't that terrible? I told her that she has to leave Rainer, of course. At first she didn't want to. But I said again and again that he won't change. A man who does such a thing once, will do it again. And she understood, finally. So I took her to father's flat. He does not sleep here very often but I have a key. I was so glad that she was safe. That was until there was a knock at our door again in the morning. This time I opened the door and it was Rainer. I slammed the door in his face. He knocked again, I opened it and then I gave him a piece of my mind; what kind of man he is and that Anna would never return to someone like him. I just wanted to slam the door again as Erich came and let him in. I couldn't believe it; I told him what kind of man Rainer is. But Erich insisted and sent me to the children. They were awake, naturally, and wanted to know

81

what was going on. I told them that Uncle Rainer and Aunt Anna had had a quarrel, just like they do. I couldn't tell them the truth. And then Erich came into the room: "Everything is alright", he said. I couldn't believe it, he went with Rainer to Anna and Rainer promised he wouldn't do it again and that was it. And Erich promised the two of them that he would put in a good word for Rainer with the town office's boss, who is a friend of his. In the end, it is a family matter, he said. You won't believe it, he was proud of his achievement. "Such things happen in the best families", he said. I was so angry with Erich but he really did not understand why. Later I talked to father about the matter. He told me it was already the fourth time, including last night, that Anna had come to him because of it all. But each time she returned to Rainer, even though he offered her his flat. For him the matter is over and done with, Anna is a grown-up and he can't force her to leave Rainer. He would love to beat Rainer up but he is too old for that. All he said about Erich was: "A leopard never changes his spots." I don't know exactly what he meant but even if I'm still a bit angry with Erich, Anna has to decide on her own what she does.

Dear Lilli, after this story I don't want to forget to tell you how nice your visit was. The children still talk about the big chocolate cake you brought with you. Even Erich ate a slice despite knowing that it was from you.

I am praying that you have a good journey.

Hugs,

Eva

Letter from Lilli to Eva 6th September 1939

Dear Eva,

It is over. All our wonderful dreams are shattered. Everything was ready. On 2nd September we had the appointment with the notary. Hans-Georg had rented a storeroom for our big pieces of furniture; all our things were packed away in cardboard boxes. We were ready for the journey. Mr Lehmann, the buyer of the shop, said that we could leave everything we don't need in the flat and that we would find an arrangement for that too. Everything was planned; directly after the appointment with the notary we were meant to give him the keys for the shop and the ones for the flat on the 15th in the morning. Hans had booked our crossing for the 15th at 12 o'clock.

Hitler is the one to blame for everything. After he declared war on Poland on the first of this month, Mr Lehmann came on the second in the morning and cancelled our deal. He said we were just postponing it. Now that there will be a war he wants to first of all await the developments and we could maybe do the deal later. But what is that now worth? Now that England is at war with Germany we won't be able to go to England. Hans is really desperate, he would love to try and sell the shop to move to South America. A former business partner from his time as an authorized signatory, a Jew, emigrated two years ago and Hans still has contact to him. Ha says he would help us at the beginning. But I cannot imagine that, it is too far away. Hans is very kind; he doesn't push me, although I feel his eagerness to take this step. The good thing in this matter is that you are staying in my life. If we were in England now, we probably couldn't have even written letters. Now everything stays as it is, except for the war. What was the reaction in the village when people heard about the war? I probably don't need to ask about Erich. It is a funny feeling that there is a war going on and still everything is the same as usual. I have to control our supply, accept orders and in the evening Hans and I unpack the boxes. The furniture should be brought back from the storeroom and into our flat within the next three days. Please forgive me, this time I hadn't got any time to prepare a parcel so I just took one of the cigar boxes and put it to the letter. Tell the children I will send chocolate soon. I hope they are well.

Hugs,
Eva

Letter from Lilli to Eva 8th September 1939

Dear Eva,

Since my last letter only two days have passed but I have to tell you this. Imagine what happened yesterday. In the morning at seven o'clock, shortly after we had opened, two men came into our shop. In the moment that they came in I had a strange feeling. They walked around the shop, had a look at everything and then they only wanted to have two packets of cigarettes. I was glad when they started to go but then they turned, looked at us and asked if we are Mr and Mrs Marten. At first we didn't answer, I don't know whether we were surprised or defiant, for they did not seem to be very polite. Then they showed us their membership cards. "Secret state police", they said like a choir. One of them said: "We have some questions", while the other one closed the shop and turned the 'Open' sign around. I felt how angry Hans was and so I took his hand and squeezed it. I then said: "Let us go upstairs to our flat, it is nicer there."

They agreed. Just as we had sat down one of them started to ask questions. Why we want to leave for England and if we dislike something in the Third Reich. Hans was marvellous, there was nothing apparent of his anger anymore when he told them we just want to go to England for one or two years to do business. After that we want to return in any case, that's why we didn't sell our furniture but rather put it into a store room. That convinced them but first we had to show them the receipt for the renting of the store room and the confirmation of the agency about the returning of the furniture. I'm so happy that we hadn't sold our furniture. At the end they asked us why we aren't members of the party and if we don't support the Führer. They gave us two forms.

84

Honestly, Eva, I don't know if I have ever been so scared before in my life. I was already imagining them leading us away. Hans says they had to have checked all lists of passengers and recognised the large amount of freight to have become suspicious. If we try and emigrate again then only with a small amount of luggage and with a return ticket then they won't be as suspicious. They have their eyes and ears everywhere. That is also the reason why I used mother's address, I don't know whether you noticed, but I used her name too. You never know whether they have still their eyes on us. Please also send your letters to mother, I see her every Sunday.

Hugs from a still frightened

Lilli

Diary entry 4th August 1945

Finally I have the energy to write down my thoughts. Erich has really made progress in the last few days. He is nearly able to use the pot without any help. The children seem to have fewer problems than I do. For me it is still hard to bear to help him out of the bed and onto the pot. Since I don't need to hold him anymore I can turn away. But Erich seems to dislike it because since I've been doing this his demand for me to help him to get into bed again when he is finished always sounds angry. Maybe he feels my disgust. But what can he expect? I do everything for him. How can I tell him my feelings? Tell him that he is a stranger to me? He abruptly interrupted all the attempts I made to talk about his escape or the war. Yesterday, I made the last attempt when I sat on the bed to clean his newly opened injuries. When I started to say something about it he turned abruptly and nearly threw me off the bed. There was such anger in his eyes. Since then I haven't spoken about it again. Yet someday he will have to talk about it, about that what has brought us to this.

Letter from Eva to Lilli 20th September 1939

Dear Lilli,

What news! I'm happy of course to know that you are staying here but for you it is so sad. For all of us the war is terrible and I would have loved it for you to be safe. I would have loved to report something else but you were right, of course, Erich is all for it. He wanted to volunteer immediately. He brushed my plea not to volunteer aside with the remark that the Führer needs him now. When I tried to remind him of his duty as a father he became really angry, for his children should be proud of him. And off he went. But then other things happened because farmer Ranft said that there are enough fighters at the moment and that Hitler needs him here now to care for the food of the army. At least he listened to him. Since then his mood has been very bad. He only lightens up a bit when he hears some good news on the radio. I don't care; at least he is still here and cannot fall, for despite all the good news, the others have weapons too.

What you have written about your 'visitors' was really frightening. How good for you to have married such an intelligent man. They would have certainly taken me with them because I wouldn't have had something to say in defence. Here it is just the same as in Hamburg; you don't notice that there is a war. Only a few boys from the village were sent to war with a little party in the town offices beforehand. The mothers and wives of them all cried, they probably weren't successful in stopping their sons and husbands either. I often ask myself what all this ado about Hitler is for, why are so many people enthusiastic about him? He's only a human. Everyone is very well but now there is a war. What is good about a war? I cannot ask Erich such things. Father is my only confidant. He said it is like back in the times of the emperor. Nobody thought any further about the war, everybody

believed that they knew everything and it is exactly the same with Hitler. Father greets you kindly, by the way, and thanks you. The children were happy, of course, when they heard that aunt Lilli is staying. Lots of love from them.
Love,
Your Eva

Letter from Lilli to Eva 3rd October 1939
Dear Eva,
Again, I don't have any good news. At the moment it feels like we are under a curse. Recently there was a notice in the newspaper that only those born between 1915 and 1917 will be enlisted for the campaign against Poland. Now Hans has received his enlistment papers in the post. At first we thought it was a mistake. Hans went to the offices responsible for our area on the same day. At first it really did seem to be a mistake. The official at the counter confirmed that only those born between 1915 and 1917 will be called upon. Yet he had to ask his superior before he would take back Hans' enlistment papers. The superior wasn't friendly at all. He asked Hans whether he had any objections to helping the Führer and the fatherland in the field. Hans didn't respond but asked politely why he was called upon, for he was not born between the dates which stood in the newspaper. They told him that they don't only need youngsters at the frontline and that because he has A-levels that he is a candidate for a higher position. Furthermore, they said that he should be proud and finally that you should never make yourself unpopular in the eyes of the Gestapo. Everything because of a passage to England and the renting of a bit more cargo hold than normal. Hans has to show up at the barracks in Hamburg at two o'clock tomorrow afternoon. I'm so afraid of tomorrow; I don't know what to say to him. I, myself am so distressed that I can't even pretend to be confident.

Hans has hired a second helper for the shop. I'm not concerned about that. I will manage. Tonight we want to go out again. Hans-Georg has reserved a table. It will be a sad evening.

Now the midday break is over, I have to wake Hans; he has had an afternoon nap. He said who knows when he will be able to do it again. Now I'm crying again. Dear Eva, please kiss the little ones from me and greet your father.

Parcel as always.

Hugs,

Your Lilli

Diary entry 16th August 1945

Today, Erich went for the first time, with my help, from our room into the kitchen. He wanted to sit down at the table. Since he's managing to keep everything down he can now drink our "Muckefuck". We have enough of that; there were so many acorns last year and the children collected them diligently. They were only caught once and then had to give their acorns away at the collecting place for animal food. I roasted the others together with grain. I'm starting to believe that our Muckefuck tastes like real coffee.

Erich still isn't talking. When he says something, it is an order for me or the children. Marie and Hildchen have already complained; they said he is so mean. They just say always 'he', when they talk about him, they are not able to say 'father'. I can understand them. Whenever they do something, it is not fast enough for him, it is not proper or they are too loud. I told them that we have to be patient; their father has been through a lot but that it is still their father. Hildchen, of course, did not agree. He is not the father she knew, he does not look like him and he does not act like him. I told her to behave, what else should I have done?

There is one ray of hope; he is crazy about the little ones. He hasn't shouted at them and when I give them something to do, he always says that one of the big ones can do it. Today, when they came home he even asked them how school was. The little ones told him everything and he seemed to like it. They are not afraid of him. After a while I sent them off into the kitchen to do their homework. Maybe this is a start.

Letter from Eva to Lilli 5th October 1939

My dear poor Lilli,

What you wrote to me made me so sad. First the matter with England and then Hans-Georg's enlistment. Really, when I talk with father about Hitler I am always very careful in case the door flies open. Who knows if it is Erich and if he has one of his comrades with him. Erich is in a really good mood again, he says that with the campaign against Poland that it is not over and that he will get his chance. You can't talk about anything else with him. He holds the opinion that he is indispensable but the local section leader Ranft, that's what he calls him, says that when the real duties come that he will let him go. It's like he's in a fever, he is working harder and longer than before, everything for the Führer and the comrades at the frontline, that's what he says.

We listen to the radio the whole day. Even when Erich is absent he wants it to run all the time so that I won't miss a message of victory. But as soon as he leaves the house I switch it off. It is no use to leave it on when I'm away, I won't hear anything. And I don't want to hear any news. A few times I have forgotten to switch the radio on in time before Erich came back home. He was really angry. But I still switch it off. Each message of victory also means that somewhere in another country there are mothers and wives who have lost their sons and husbands for this victory. Even in our village it happened to one mother, her son was hit by a piece of shrapnel. At the same time they

say in the radio, the victorious German army has suffered no losses.
The leader of the NSDAP for our area personally went to her and told
her the news. It is said, that she answered that she is proud of him
because he died for the Führer and the fatherland. Such words travel
fast. Can a mother really think something like that?

Dear Lilli, I actually wanted to cheer you up but the war is so terrible,
I pray every evening for your Hans. Since the war has started I've
started praying again in the mornings. Erich does not believe in these
things. This may be the only thing you have in common with him. I
think about the words of our pastor frequently, he once said in a
sermon: "In moments of hopelessness you find god."

You may not believe in it but it comforts me and I pray every evening
now with the little ones before they sleep. Erich always grumbles but I
do it even then.

The children are very well; they say they wanted to have a picnic with
their aunt Lilli again. Your parcel this time was nearly shaming for
me. The tasty liqueur for me and the cigars and the brandy for my
father. And not to mention the sweets for the children. Thank you so
much, dear Lilli, also from father. Many hugs and if you don't manage
to come here soon then I will visit you in Hamburg.

Yours,

Eva

Diary entry 30th August 1945

Today it is five weeks ago that Erich came back. And today he took
his first steps alone. I hope he makes further progress then I can put
the pot into the kitchen in a few days and maybe he will manage the
way across the yard in two or three weeks. That would really be a
blessing. It will be colder soon and I can't keep the window open
the whole day then. He only speaks to me and the big ones about
the essentials or he grumbles at me and the children. The food

never has the right temperature, it is not right when the big ones are present. He turns them out into the kitchen most of the time. When they want to go out after six o'clock in the evening he forbids it. It is not acceptable for girls at their age to roam around outside at that time. They should never think it will carry on like before, now that he is back home. Sometimes he says it outright: "Your mother is far too soft, she always was, now I'm taking over the regiment again."

Regiment. How much I hate this word. Hasn't he learnt anything? The war is over. Sometimes I wish he wouldn't have come back.

I'm going to the Ranft's soon.

Letter from Hans-Georg to Lilli 8th October 1939

My beloved Lilli,

Finally I've manage to write to you. I'm very well. Everything turned out to be very bureaucratic. At first I had to go to a fitting then the company commander gave me the marching orders for the next day. The next day we went by train in the direction of Poland. During the trip I was able to sleep most of the time if the comrades weren't singing too loudly. Among the normal soldiers I am probably the oldest. When we arrived at our destination everything was quiet. Generally, I haven't seen or heard any fighting so far. We are in a small Polish village not too far from the border. When we arrived the village was empty except for some pioneers. Everything was deserted. Our job is to protect the village. Now it is getting dark. I have a room in a farm together with a comrade. He is from Kiel and very nice. It is amazing, everyone here is very poor, but despite that it is still very cosy. I will go to bed soon because at midnight I am on guard for the first time. I have to orientate myself by watching and asking the others concerning my duty because they have already had two years training. I haven't even had an introduction. I'm sure I'll manage not to attract attention though. At the moment I'm sitting on the bed and asking myself who has slept in this room before. I imagine the owner coming in tonight and asking: "Who came into my house and who is sleeping in my bed?" Just like in the fairy tale of Snow White. I hope you are well and that you haven't got any problems in the shop. I know you will manage. Who else is as strong? I'm so proud of you. Please don't worry about me, everything is quiet here. Please don't send anything to me either, the rations are really good. I would be happy if you write to me. My beloved Lilli, I miss you so much, I hope we will see each other again soon.

With love,

Hans

Letter from Lilli to Eva 15th October 1939

Dear Eva,

Today, I received the first letter from Hans. He reported that he was, as soon as he arrived, fitted out and moved to a regiment. The next morning they went to Poland by train. Luckily all actions of fighting were over in Poland. Hans has to protect an area with his comrades where no fighting is taking place. I can feel that Hans is suffering very much under these circumstances. I shouldn't send anything to Hans, he says he is well and the rations are sufficient. I will still send him some of the hazelnuts covered with chocolate which he likes so much, of course. I am happy that Hans is safe. I don't know what will happen in the next weeks and months but I'm not giving up the hope to see Hans in good shape again soon.

Everything is normal in the shop, I am managing to do the work and in the evenings I fall exhausted into bed, so I haven't got much time to think. That's a good thing. Today it is Sunday and I've managed to pull myself together so that I can write this long overdue letter to you. I hope you and the little ones are well. Please greet your father. Parcel

as always.
Love and hugs,
Your Lilli

Letter from Eva to Lilli 20th October 1939

Dear Lilli,

Your letter made me happy. It seems to be the truth that they are speaking of on the radio. The German troops have hardly had any problems with resistance actually. I keep that in mind; they are repeating it all the time. Perhaps the war will be over soon. It is really a blessing to hear that Hans is of a sound condition. May god allow that it will stay like that. I hardly see Erich, if he is not working then he is sitting together with his party members in the offices. And when he is present he just talks about the glorious victories of the German army. Even the children miss him. Last Sunday he was finally at home the whole day to take care of the proper education of the children, he said. Imagine, he used the time to teach the big ones the 'Horst-Wessel-Song'. Hildchen has learnt it very fast, Marie needed some more time. Erich was a bit impatient but Hildchen helped her sister. Erich didn't notice but the little ones chuckled. For the children it was a nice day and when I put them to bed they were happy. They said that father should come and say goodnight too. They haven't asked for that for weeks. After the children were asleep we drank a bottle of wine and Erich didn't talk about the war or the party. It was just like it used to be.

Father is well like always, he still seems to be happy with Mrs Trapp. She is really a very nice woman. Yesterday, father invited me and the children to his house for coffee. Mrs Trapp had baked an apple cake. It was a nice afternoon. We played 'Mensch ärgere Dich nicht' with the children. Marie and Hilde both won once. Father pretended to be really annoyed about it. We laughed so much. Next week I will invite the two of them to our house and I will invite Anna too. Rainer has forbidden her to visit us but she says that he is always in the pub in the afternoon now that he has lost his job. She is really going through difficult times with her husband.

Father greets you kindly and thanks you.

Kisses from the children.

Hugs,

Your Eva

Letter from Hans-Georg to Lilli 12th June 1940

My beloved Lilli,

I apologise for not having written for so long. But everything happened so quickly. At eight o'clock in the morning we got our marching orders. Marching off in two hours. To France. You read that right, I'm now stationed in France. Sadly it is not as quiet here as in Poland. We are behind the frontline but we are being attacked by partisans all the time. They attack and in the next moment they are gone. You know I planned not to shoot any men but to rather shoot above the hostile lines but this is impossible when I have to protect my comrades. I don't know how many men I have killed but when we pass a shot Frenchman I always ask myself whether I am responsible for his death.

Dear Lilli, it is so terrible not to be able to talk to anyone about it. Nearly all of the comrades ridicule the fallen and some steal from them. Sometimes I think I see remorse in their faces for a short moment but this instant is always so short that I ask myself whether I was wrong. I don't dare to talk to them about it.

Sadly there is another thing; I have been promoted to the rank sergeant. I don't understand how this happened. I always tried to be reserved and not to attract attention. I assume that they chose me because I'm the eldest in this group. Now I feel even more responsible for these cruel actions.

Dear Lilli, many thanks for the pralines. I ate only one. I shared the others. Many don't get any parcels. I am the most grateful for your letters. When I see your handwriting and read your words you are so near. I'm very glad that you're managing the shop so well. Please greet your mother from me and say thank you for her help. Wouldn't it make sense if she were to move in with you? I hope that I will get some holiday soon; some comrades who started in Poland are on their way home for one week. I hope to see you soon.

With love,

Hans

Letter from Lilli to Eva 14th June 1940

Dear Eva,

It was so long ago that I received your last letter but I've had so much to do. It is really rather amazing; although we're in the middle of a war I have to do more than ever. You would never believe how many celebrations people, especially the party, organise. They only want the best. I always have to say to myself, Lilli, keep your mouth shut. But it really is very strange; in the newspapers and the radio they always talk about wartime economy and renunciation. Everybody who does not buy German products is seen as being non-German. But these gentlemen order French Cognac, Russian caviar and delicacies from all over the world. Mother often helps me with the preparation of the platters and with the deliveries. She then stays overnight with me. I like it, it is nice not to be alone in this large flat at night.

Hans has been ordered to go to France in the meantime. Sadly, it is not as quiet there as it is in Poland; they have to fight partisans all the time. You have surely heard about it on the radio. Hans has been promoted to the rank sergeant but he is not at all happy about it. He has got the feeling that he is now even more guilty and responsible for what happens there. I always try and write comforting things to him but there is nothing left other than to write about the shop and about you and the children. He knows me too well.

Dear Eva, I'm glad to know that Erich is still with you. It is so strange; he does not know how happy he should be. How Hans would love to be in his situation.

Greet your father and hugs for the children.

Hugs,

Lilli

Letter from Hans to Lilli 20ᵗʰ June 1940

Dear Lilli,

Today was the worst day of all. We surprised some of the partisans in a camp and arrested them. They were very young, nearly children, the eldest not older than eighteen. And there was also one girl. You already know that partisans are no regular soldiers. Our commander picked out the eldest and asked him where the rest of them are hiding. When he answered in French, the commander could not understand anything and so he came to me: "Marten, you have A-levels, what did he say?"

I translated it for him. Then I got the order to ask him about his fellow conspirators, that's what the commander called them. He refused to answer. The commander became angry and slapped him with his binoculars in the face, right in front of my eyes.

"Marten, you will surely volunteer to free us from this scum."

This is the order for one of us to put together a firing squad of volunteers. At first I wasn't able to say anything and then I answered: "I can't do it, commander." He went red, looked at me and said he could give me the order to do it. When I didn't answer, he snarled at private Hannig: "Then you do it again, Hannig." He subsequently turned and went away. Hannig is a nice guy actually but he always says when he looks for someone for this order: "Do you think that they would treat you differently?" Generally, he needn't look for volunteers. Those who take part get always privileges, sometimes even one day special leave. I know other commanders give a direct order and pick the firing squad by themselves. I don't know what I would do then. Refusal would mean refusal to obey orders and that would mean military court. For today I managed to avoid it. But I showed the commander up, who, in his eyes, wanted to give me a privilege. I don't know how he will react.

Lilli, I can't stand it anymore, knowing now that I probably won't get a holiday. I miss you so much. Your reason, your honesty and your kind face. Dear Lilli, please write to me and maybe add another bar of chocolate. When I open a bar of chocolate it always gives off the wonderful scent just like the sweet corner in our shop. I always tell my comrades where you can find this special delicacy in our shop and on which shelf it is. We enthuse together about noble pralines, tasty peppermint and of course about the different nuts covered in chocolate. We wonder then what you will send the next time. In these moments it is just as if I'm there. The comrades feel the same; when one of them gets a cake or home-made wine from home they report every detail about how their mothers or wives produced these things. They even look happy in these short moments. I cannot write anymore, I'm becoming too sad.

I love you so much; the thought of you keeps me alive.

With love,

Hans

Diary entry 10th September 1945

I'm almost embarrassed. The children and Erich are sleeping and I'm sitting here in front of the contents of the parcel which I received for my work. Today, I stacked wood and peat into the interior of the house for the winter. At the moment I'm working alone. Old Mrs Ranft just gives me orders and I work them off. Mrs Ranft has suffered from rheumatism the last weeks so she is not able to control me all the time. Today, she said to me that I have to bring all the fuel from outside, inside. You never know when it gets cold and she, especially with her rheumatism, needs a warm surrounding. It was four o'clock in the afternoon and at ten o'clock in the evening I still hadn't finished. I would have probably worked into the night if Mr Ranft hadn't come and helped me. When we finished at twelve o'clock he invited me into the kitchen for a cup of coffee. At first I wanted to refuse but he said we deserve one. Coffee, I had never thought he meant real coffee, real filtered coffee. It was like heaven. I felt like I did before the war. I will never write that Muckefuck tastes like coffee again! We just talked the time away about the war. He told me how he experienced the war in England. How many friends of his abandoned him at the beginning of the war. How he was allowed to stay, despite the war, to do further work in agriculture. Such a thing would be impossible in Germany. How Erich always talked about the 'Tommies' who only deserve to be dead. Mr Ranft says that after the war his mother wrote to him to tell him that his father had fallen. He had to come; otherwise the farm would be taken over by the English. So he came and they entrusted him with the farm. Now it is half past one and I can hardly believe my luck. Four pig trotters, two pork joints and enough potatoes for one meal. How Erich loved to eat 'swinspoten', that's what he called them. I'm still not tired; the coffee is keeping me awake. So I'm going to use the time to marinate the joints and the trotters. Tomorrow there will be a banquet; maybe this will cheer Erich up a bit.

Letter from Eva to Lilli 12th July 1941

Dear Lilli,

Now it has happened, Erich has been enlisted. He says now that the Führer will show his power to the bolshevists, he has to do his duty. Even Mr Ranft hasn't held him back this time. He's gone so far as to give him a letter of recommendation as local section leader and as his employer. Tomorrow, he has to go to Hamburg and then directly to Russia. I worry so much but Erich is happy. It seems as if his dearest wish has now come true after a long time of waiting. The children are despondent; they don't want to lose their father. They have heard a lot about the war in school and what an honour it is to fight for the Führer and the fatherland. But they also saw how children were fetched by their mothers because their fathers had fallen. The teachers always say how proud these children should be, for their father has died a heroic death. Hildchen said that she does not want to be proud of her father; she wants him to stay here. I had tears in my eyes but Erich just said that there are things she does not understand yet and that she shouldn't say something like that. Then he went to his comrades, to celebrate the farewell. He said I shouldn't wait up for him. But today I can't be angry with him. I will wait for him; I want to spend the last few hours with him when he comes back. Finally now I know how you felt when Hans was called up and I know that it will get far worse. May god allow our husbands to come back from the war.

It is nice that your mother helps you and comforts you. I'm so happy to know father is here too. Mrs Trapp is very important now for the children. They visit father very often and play with them both. She never had any children but she has the same good feel for children like you. The children miss you, they often say: "When is aunt Lilli going to come?"

I hope we see each other soon. It's been such a long time. When Erich

is at war it will be easier. Thank you from father and of course from me for your last parcel.
Kind regards,
Your Eva

Letter from Erich to Eva 15ᵗʰ July 1941

My dear wife,

I am writing to report what a great event this operation is for the Führer and the people. The comrades in the barracks gave me a warm welcome. I heard that the volunteers have a very good standing here. Anyway, I was only here for the fitting out and to receive my marching orders, finally. Now I'm sitting together with I don't know how many comrades to get to the frontline. In my wagon there are more quiet comrades because no one is singing here. Most of them are reading something. From the other compartments you can hear our songs all the time. Most of the time the 'Horst-Wessel-Song', but they are even singing 'Die Fahne hoch'. I would love to change the compartment, but who knows whether there is a seat for me. I can hardly wait to get to the frontline to give the Russians a good going over.

Now I'm going to try to sleep a bit, I've been awake since four o'clock this morning. Please greet Marie, Hilde and the little ones from their father.

Kind regards,
Your husband, Erich

Letter from Erich to Eva 20ᵗʰ July 1941

My dear wife,

I'm finally with my comrades at the frontline. We have a safe position from which our missions are commanded. It is unbelievable what the Führer is achieving. He has the overview of all these missions. We just follow his orders. I just heard shellfire. It is our artillery which is putting pressure on the Ivan, that's what they call the Russians here. It sounds lovelier than music to me. I'm part of the next platoon. Now I can sleep for three hours. My watch starts at midnight together with my bunk neighbour, Heinz Winkler, a Bavarian.

Please send my greetings to Marie and Hilde and to the little ones from their father.

Kind regards,

Your husband, Erich

Letter from Eva to Erich 1st August 1941

My dear Erich,

I was glad to hear from you so soon. I beg you to be careful for the sake of the children. The children and I are well. I just received a ration card for a new winter coat for Marie. They refused the one for Hildchen, she can wear Marie's old coat. It is still okay, I just have to sew on two patches on the elbows. Father has started to work again; he's helping at the bakery in the mornings. You know, his assistant is at the front too. Father hopes to get some extra bread for us. But until now he hasn't managed to get anything. Shall I send you one of your thick work pullovers before the winter or do you need something else? Love from the children.

With love, Eva

Letter from Erich to Eva 1st October 1941

My dear wife,

Today I had to pass on the message of the advancement of our troops to the commander from a lookout using a radio. I would have loved to have been fighting with the comrades who gave the Ivan a good going over. But our radio operator was hit by a piece of shrapnel directly in the eye. So I received the order to make the announcements for the commander. Actually, it is not important where I do my duty for the Führer. It is an honour to take part in the operation. Yesterday, we were able to listen to a broadcast of the Führer himself during a fighting pause. He spoke directly to us. I was so proud. The commander gave the order afterwards to sing together 'Die Fahne hoch'. It is sad, we would have done it immediately and without order back then. But some of us don't understand the great aim that we have due to Hitler. It is really wonderful to see how far we have marched in such a short time. It feels like we are invincible. The few comrades who have fallen make no difference considering the thousands of Ivans we have caught. If it goes on like this it won't take long and the Russian army will have to surrender.

I hope everything is alright at home. After your last letter I have to beg you urgently to only apply for ration cards when it is really necessary. We need all our reserve supplies for the war. I sent you some of my cigarettes for your father. I give most of them to my smoking comrades, of course. If it is possible please send me a few pairs of warm socks and my warm work pullover. Not the blue one, the green one. And it would be nice to have a comb too.

Greet Marie, Hilde and the little ones from their father.

Kind regards , your husband, Erich

Letter from Hans to Lilli 1st November 1941

Dear Lilli,

Sometimes miracles really happen. Imagine, our commander was posted to Africa because of his service here, they say. I'm trying not to render outstanding services after what I've heard about going to Africa. Perhaps this order has saved my life because after the incident which I've written to you about, I was always placed in unknown areas in the front row of the advance. This is the most dangerous part. Two comrades were shot near me by partisans in the last few weeks. Now the ceasefire agreement is already one year old and we are still fighting far behind the former frontline. Our radio operator, a great guy, managed to arrange that we can listen to the radio sometimes. These are nice moments, especially when we can listen to the request program with the greetings from home. There have been greetings for one of our comrades three times. But the last one was very sad because the private Sabrowski, for whom the greeting was, was killed one week before during an attack by the partisans. That was really awful but actually it is quieter here than in other parts and especially quieter than in Africa where they are fighting actively. Sadly, I heard that the campaign against Russia has started. I just don't know how this should all end?

But there is good news too. The new commander seems to be a nice guy, maybe I will get a little home leave this year. If I'm lucky it might be for Christmas or at the turn of the year. Or maybe earlier.

In happy anticipation.

I love you,

Hans

Letter from Erich to Eva 17th December 1941

My dear wife,

I can report to you with pride that I was promoted to a private first class. I'm not quite sure but I think it has something to do with our last attack. We shot towards the bunkers of the Ivan, ready to attack with our shellfire and when their gunfire ceased, I ran with a handful of comrades to the bunkers to place explosives in them. We blew up one bunker after the other. The Ivans inside tried to stop us with their rifles but after one bunker was blown up we advanced without them seeing us. The bunkers are set up in the way that one of them covers an area and when one is gone, the others aren't able to see everything. Those in the bunkers were surely surprised when they all of a sudden exploded.

Now I'm a private first class and additionally I have received one week holiday. At first I thought that I wouldn't be able to leave the comrades alone but our commander said that he needs well rested soldiers and that I deserve the holiday. You can expect me in one week. Please greet Marie, Hilde and the little ones from their father. I will bring you something too. Concerning my clothes, they arrived here. Please prepare all the winter clothes that I have. I want to take them with me when I return to the comrades.

Kind regards,

Your Erich

Letter from Lilli to Eva 20th December 1941

My dear Eva,

Hans-Georg has to leave for Russia as well now. During his home leave he sold some soap to Mrs Rosenthal, you know, one of our neighbours whose shop was destroyed by the SS in 1938. Whoever watched didn`t hesitate for long. The next day we found his marching orders to the Russian front line in our letterbox. On the same day he had to register in Hamburg at his new unit, not as a sergeant, but as private Marten. Enclosed was his demotion because of non-Aryan behaviour and also the order to remove his insignia at once. And I had so been looking forward to a Christmas with Hans.

I wish you a merry Christmas. I hope you have had better news from Erich.

Please be in touch as soon as possible

Hugs,

Your Lilli

Letter from Hans to Lilli 4th January 1942

Dear Lilli,

Today, I am finally managing to write to you. There was really no chance earlier. Since I arrived in Russia we have been moving all the time. Every time we have had to set up a new camp and that is a big job with all this snow around. On my way I passed many destroyed villages. Often you see dead Russians lying in ditches at the side of the road. From time to time you see more cruel images. There are men and women hanging from trees without their clothes, only in underwear and with a sign saying 'saboteur' on their chest. It is so terrible. These people have only tried to protect their homes and their families. I know that these people are right and that we are committing a crime here. In France it only happened rarely but here there are sometimes quarrels when comrades fight over the belongings of fallen Russians. Perhaps the Führer should have taken a winter holiday in Russia before he started a war here. I shouldn't write like this but I somehow have to express what I feel. Please throw this letter into the fire after reading it. You never know whether the Gestapo will visit you again. That's also the reason why I am writing to your mother's address. I hope she is by your side. That would comfort me. Please greet her kindly from me. I miss you so much. I don't know what I'd do without you. I would have loved to have spent Christmas with you.

With love,

Hans

Diary entry 12th September 1945

It is getting worse from day to day. I had hoped Erich would take part in our life again after some time. But now I don't believe in it any more. Yesterday, he nearly hit Marie, he has never done such a thing before. She hadn't done any harm. There was an English officer in her school to tell the children what terrible things Hitler has done. Marie asked me at home why Hitler attacked so many countries. I wasn't able to answer because Erich jumped out of the bed. He shouted at her that she shouldn't talk about the Führer in this way and he raised his hand. If I hadn't interfered he would have hit her. I sent Marie out of the room then. Erich was very exhausted after that but he said I should count myself lucky that he is still not healthy. It sounded like a threat. The rest of the day he didn't talk and he refused to eat anything. Marie cried very hard afterwards. I wanted to comfort her but it seemed senseless to repeat the same thing over and over again. But I did it all the same: "He is your father; he still needs time to get used to everything again."

She just stared at me uncomprehendingly. Am I a bad mother if I ask my children for understanding? I have to protect the children from him. I will ask old Mrs Schulz to stay with the children when I'm at the Ranft's farm.

Letter from Eva to Lilli 6th January 1942
Dear Lilli,

Your letter really made me think about everything again. What injustice Hitler is committing! I didn't have much time to ponder because Erich returned on home leave on the same day that your letter arrived. You already know that I can't talk about such things with him. Erich hasn't changed; he only talks about how good things are. And he even told the children about the frontline and about the good comradeship. The children listened excitedly. Only once I was shocked. Hildchen asked whether they shoot men dead. But Erich didn't get angry, he took Hildchen and Marie onto his lap and explained to them that that has to be done, otherwise the Russians would shoot him. Then he asked them whether they want that. They both hugged him and said no. It was moving to see how he sat there with our daughters.

Dear Lilli, our Christmas was really nice, even Anna was here. Since

Rainer has also been enlisted we have been seeing each other regularly. She does not talk about her relationship to Rainer but I have the feeling that the longer he is away, the better she feels. We all were so thankful for your parcel. I don't know how you manage to send all these things to us without ration cards. Ours are never enough. It was so wonderful, to put some sweets under the Christmas tree for the children. Can you believe it, Erich pinched some chocolate from the children on Christmas Eve as we were all sitting together. The children were outraged but laughed at the same time about their 'sweet' father. Even father was very happy about another ration of tobacco. He is now also smoking his cigar stubs in his pipe. For a while the children collected cigar stubs and cigarette ends for him, especially from in front of our pub. But this is senseless now; nobody throws these remains away anymore. I often see smokers collecting their stubs in a small tin box at the bus station.

The three days that Erich was with us were really nice, especially for the children. I often thought sadly about your letter but Erich didn't notice. On Christmas Eve in the evening when father and Anna were gone, we put the children to bed and drank a bottle of wine together like we used to. It was the last one which we had in the cellar from the time before the war. Then Erich gave me a small silver brooch and told me that he would be returning to the front the next morning as he does not want to leave his comrades alone anymore. Two days before the end of his holiday! I just nodded. What should I have said? I couldn't have changed his mind and I didn't want to spoil his last evening. Yesterday morning he crept into the girls' room and kissed them goodbye, whispered merry Christmas and went away. He forbade me to accompany him to the bus. So we said goodbye at the front door. I really hope Erich takes care of himself. May god have an eye on our husbands, for they are both in Russia. Imagine, they called upon farmer Ranft in November. Before that he was indispensable as

the mayor and as a farmer. I heard that his wife will be taking over the farm as her son remained in England at the start of the war. Dear Lilli, I wish you and your mother a happy new year despite the war.
With love,
Your Eva

Letter from Hans-Georg to Lilli 10th February 1942

Dear Lilli,

Now it is February already. It is still so cold. We can't complain about not having enough snow. This is rather bad because we moved three times in the last three weeks. Every time we arrived we thought that there would be peace and quiet at last. But then the next order always came to set off again. Up to now I have been lucky, our unit has to protect and we are not directly at the front. Everything has been quiet except for some small attacks. But I think that it is only a matter of time until we have to go to the frontline too. It must be terrible there. The lorries full of injured soldiers drive through our camps on their way to the military hospital behind us. The platoon won't stop.

Anyway dear Lilli, I have got good news this time too. I found someone to talk with in an open way. Johannes Huber, a private from Munich. Whilst building the last camp we started to talk. Johannes cursed loudly about the Führer when he sank into the snow with a tent. He didn't notice that I was behind him. He was shocked. But I laughed and since that moment we've been spending a great deal of time together. It helps to talk openly about the madness of the war and about Hitler and his people. We often ask ourselves which of the comrades think the same. We are sure that there are more than we believe. Johannes has got an electrical shop in Munich. He told me that the Gestapo came to his shop and wanted a list of all persons who had bought a 'Radio Super'. These persons were to be observed because it is easy to listen to the enemy broadcasts with these sets.

After that he sent a letter to all buyers with the message that listening to enemy broadcasts is forbidden, even if it is easy with the radios they bought and that the Gestapo had just visited him and had an eye on these radios. He even wrote "in the name of the Führer". But that was not enough; one of the customers had to be one of them, one of the party. One week after sending the letters he had his marching orders to the Russian frontline in his letterbox together with a refusal of all supply contracts for electrical equipment.

Dear Lilli, you can imagine why I am writing this to you. Our 'Saba' is one of these radios. The Gestapo is interested in them so please be careful. You do not make only me happy with your parcels. We share everything here except our opinions. But I hope this will change among our ordinary ranks. Have you heard something about Mrs Rosenthal? Is she still there?

Dear Lilli, I miss you.

With love,

Hans

Letter from Lilli to Eva 20th February 1942

Dear Eva,

I'm glad that you and the children had Erich with you for a few days. It seems as if Erich will never change with his returning to the front earlier! At first I wanted to write: Only Erich does such thing! But I can report to you that I heard the same thing from women in the shop. I thought about it and the comrades are probably like family in this difficult time. So don't be too sad. Hans-Georg has written that he is well at the moment. He is not directly at the front.

Have you gone recently into the cellar because of an air-raid warning? There is no air-raid shelter near to you, is there? We should go to an air-raid shelter if possible but even here there aren't enough and they are often too far away. I heard that the shelters are often only for the higher members of the party and their families. The occupants of our house flee into the cellar under the shop when the sirens start. I always have a little bar of chocolate kept there for the little children. I want to distract them. It seems to work. This morning, little Lisa from above our flat said to me: "I hope there will be another alarm then we will get chocolate again!"

I, myself, am not afraid of the bombs, I think of Hans in these moments. I'm sure that he would prefer to be in my shoes. Mother has been living with me now since January. It is really rather practical because without her help I wouldn't be able to manage all the work. The matter with the ration cards is easy to explain. There are two reasons. At first concerning our tobacco products, spirits and sweets; I have a considerable supply in our flat, which Hans and I started as a private reserve long before the war. These things don't appear on any delivery list. Secondly, the wealthier gentlemen are not tiring of having one celebration after the other. So I receive deliveries for the platters with specialties, alcohol and sweets, which other shops don't get anymore. But who can control whether all the pralines and all the specialties which I ordered are on the platters? Which is not to mention the remains of the food, which I just take with me anyway. It is a bit embarrassing that I'm still so well off but I always put more products in those customers' bags who have many children, more than they should get with their ration cards. Dear Eva, so for you again I have included a small parcel. Nonetheless, I still notice the war here too. Today a captain came and took our big car. The car will now be used for the service of the Reich, he said, and he left me with a confiscation certificate. I can then claim my property back after the war. Even the other one will be taken in a few days. So I called one leading person who uses our services for his endless celebrations and informed him that I won't be able to deliver the platters from next week on anymore. When he heard the reason he just said he would

sort it. I assume I will be able to keep the car for a little while longer.
Please hug the children and greet your father.
Kind regards,
Your Lilli

Diary entry 20th September 1945

I thought it couldn't get worse, but the better Erich feels, the more he tries to make decisions concerning our life. He is so stubborn, every time I oppose his ideas he insults me. The children don't dare to enter our room, except to sleep. If they do, he chases them away by shouting at them without a reason or he says abruptly that they should disappear into the kitchen. He no longer treats any of the children differently. Today he said to me that he no longer wants me working for a traitor. How could I dare to work for such a person? I tried to explain to him that he would have died without the food from farmer Ranft. "I would rather die than allow someone to help me, who supported English!"

Erich was so angry when he said that and looked at me as if I am his enemy. This afternoon I will have to explain this to Mr Ranft. I will tell him the truth, even if I speak ill of my own husband. What other options have I got?

Diary entry 21st September 1945

Mr Ranft was entirely shocked. He didn't want to believe it. Only when I described Erich's behaviour did he start to nod. I started to cry so he took me into his arms and comforted me. "It will get better and Erich still needs time." I felt so silly. It was exactly what I always told the children. What is even worse is that I enjoyed this embrace. No man other than Erich has ever embraced me. I know it is not right, I am a married woman.

I have the feeling that Erich's reaction when I came home was my punishment. When he saw the package that farmer Ranft gave to me as a goodbye, he totally lost his temper. He attacked me, tore the package out of my hand and threw it on the floor. He shouted: "I already told you, I would rather die than take something from him!"

When I tried to collect the valuable food he pulled me up by the wrist and shouted at old Mrs Schulz that she should take the food as payment for her work as nanny and that she does not need to come again. She was so frightened. She collected the food and quickly left. I was glad that the children were in the kitchen but they must have heard everything. Then Erich lay down on the bed exhausted. He is really strong again. I often think; why is he back? I am becoming less and less ashamed for such thoughts. If only Lilli could be here, if I only had an address to write to and not only this diary which leaves me alone with my thoughts.

Letter from Erich to Eva 1st October 1942

My dear wife,

I can tell you that our campaign is progressing well. However, we haven't been able to advance as quickly as in the past months. The Ivans are defending themselves well. It will be their final resistance before the final defeat. We are fighting more determinedly for the Führer and fatherland, even though this sometimes means we have to make sacrifices. Our losses have decreased since we captured a crowd of Russian Jews. Now we don't have to do the dirty jobs anymore. They now have to dig up the fighting positions whilst they are under fire. When the Ivans shoot their own men it is even better, that is no great loss. Despite the weather not appearing to be on the side of the Führer, I am sure that we will soon have the victory.

Send me some underwear, mine is useless after the double wearing in the winter.

Kind regards,
Your husband Erich

Letter from Eva to Lilli 1st December 1942
Dear Lilli,

Many thanks for your last parcel. Although we are not suffering from poverty your parcels are always a welcome pleasure. The children are well. You mustn't have a bad conscience. I know you; you help other people more than you have told me. You deserve to be well off; you have worked so hard for your shop. I can't report anything new about Erich. He has written that all is well at the frontline and he has not written about defeats or withdrawal, even if such things are often whispered here.

Lilli, I discovered something terrible: There is something engraved on the back of the brooch that Erich gave to me to say goodbye. I wasn't able to read it and I showed it to father, he says he can't read it either but that it is Russian writing. Now I think about it all the time; where did Erich find it? Somehow I don't want to know.

Dear Lilli, I have enclosed it in this letter. I am sure you know someone who could use it to swap it for food. I don't want it anymore. When Erich asks about it I will tell him I lost it. What else can I do? He would never understand. There were only two bomb alarms here so far. But sometimes we hear gunfire when the weather is clear. I assume it is your air defence.

Father and Mrs Trapp are well. The children call her grandma and I call her by her first name. Her name is Lieselotte. I have to tell you another very sad story. Mrs Salbei is dead. She cut her wrists open after she had heard about the death of her husband. He fell in Africa. This war only tells terrible stories. They were only together for such a short time. I thank God that our two husbands are still alive. I pray for them every day.

113

Dear Lilli, I hope you and your mother are well. Kind regards from the children.
Hugs,
Your Eva

Letter from Hans to Lilli 20ᵗʰ March 1943
Dear Lilli,

It is five o'clock in the morning and pitch dark. Except for the flares, which the Russians fire towards our position regularly. Apart from that everything is quiet. I'm on guard and have a moment of peace now so that I can write a few lines to you, my love. It is so very cold here. I have to put away the pencil every now and then to warm my fingers up on the oven in the guard room. But I don't want to complain, I know about many units who haven't got any fuel anymore or only have enough to light a fire for a few hours. We are lucky here, the ovens are burning day and night. In the last few weeks there has been a lot of bad news. The whole sixth army has been defeated in Stalingrad by the Russians. The survivors have all been taken prisoner. People have been saying that nearly all of the generals and higher ranked officers were flown out of the area. I don't know whether it is the truth but I wouldn't be surprised.

We have withdrawn twice now. The enemy broke through again and again and so we had to close our lines by withdrawal. I think if Hitler and his people have really lost a whole army then they won't be able to win the war anymore. Only, what about us? Will we all be taken prisoner by the Russians or will we be forced to fight until the last man is dead, like some of the officers say it. The same officers who are flown out when it becomes dangerous.

Lilli, how could it come so far? The Schnapps you put in your last parcel was a blessing. How often we were able to warm ourselves with the grog thanks to you. Sadly, the bottle is empty. If it is possible, please send another bottle with the next parcel. I hope I will receive it because I don't believe that we will be staying here for a long time. I think of you in every free minute that I have; sometimes I have the feeling that I can see you standing in the shop behind the counter. These are the best moments for me and I wish they would never end. I have to stop now, there is a changing of the guard soon and they shouldn't catch me writing private post whilst I am on duty. The worse the war is, the harder we are punished for small offences. It is as if the higher ranks are making us responsible for their failure.

Dear Lilli, I love you,

Hans

Letter from Hans to Lilli 27ᵗʰ March 1943

Dear Lilli,

I wrote to you the last time a few days ago and now I have found the time to write again. I'm in the same situation as last time. It is five o'clock in the morning and the sun will rise in a few hours. I am writing now because I am not sure when I will get the chance again. Tomorrow, we have to advance to the frontline and there it is more dangerous. I have to tell you something. Yesterday evening, one of our comrades was collected and taken away. The sergeant told us to line up afterwards and then explained the reason. Comrade Ziegler is to go on trial at the military court because of treason. Can you believe what he did! In a letter to his wife he doubted the victory and called Hitler names. The captain said that Ziegler will probably be lucky and will just go to prison because he did his duty so well. I think the sergeant put in a good word for him. He is alright. I once talked to him privately during a guard watch. He is a university man; he studied philosophy and history and worked as a teacher before the war, that is until they enlisted him.

Dear Lilli, I keep all of your letters. I always carry them with me. I hope you have given my letters the warmth they deserve and that you did not use them to light the fire. I, myself, am putting another piece of wood into the oven in this moment to warm my fingers.

The war is progressing even better than I told you in my last letter. Johannes Huber is now a real friend of mine, I can always talk with him about the heroic deeds of the German army, about the few losses we have had and about the certain victory which won't take long. The bottle you sent me is empty again but this time I didn't drink it together with the comrades. I gave it to one comrade who was hit and couldn't be taken to the military hospital on the same night. He was in so much pain and we hadn't got any medicine anymore, so we gave him the bottle of rum for the night. That calmed him down and he was still peaceful when the medics fetched him. But all the same he sadly died yesterday.

Dear Lilli, I hope you are still well and optimistic. If you still have something left then please send it to the wife of Johannes, she has to care for three children and they are not so well off. I enclose the address. I have to stop now, same situation as last time. I miss you so much. This year I won't get a holiday. Now that we are so close to victory all leave has been cancelled.

I love you,
Hans

Letter from the wife of Johannes Huber to Lilli 10th June 1943
Dear Mrs Marten,

I want to thank you so much for the marvellous package. It really helped us, for our shop is not making any profit anymore. I gave the boys half a bar of chocolate, they were all excited. I will change the rest for food. My Heiner wrote a lot about your Hans-Georg, they are helping each other in this terrible war. It must be worse in Hamburg than here. So I hope you are well and thank you again.

Yours sincerely
Maria Huber

Letter from Lilli to Eva 20th November 1943

Dear Eva,

Yesterday, they fetched Mrs Rosenthal. They came early in the morning and took her and the children. I saw it all because I was just arriving at the shop with my morning delivery. Every time I secretly gave her some food over the wall in the yard after closing time, I begged her to flee or to hide. But she always said: "Where should we hide? It is too late to flee." And with the children. She has got two; I think they are the same age as Marie and Hildchen. I'm so ashamed; I should have hidden them but I was too afraid. Now they are on their way to one of the camps. May the god you believe in allow them to survive.

Apart from that I have good news. Last week, two letters came from Hans and he is well. He can't write in an open way anymore, they imprisoned a comrade who wrote badly about Hitler. But he made me understand how he sees the situation. They are all withdrawing and he hopes that the war is over soon. Sadly his unit received the order to go directly to the frontline. Anyway, I hope for the best. Have you heard anything from Erich, is he well too? How are you and your father? The war is wearing mother out. There are so many alarms, again and again, and then we have to go into the cellar for hours. We are only allowed to flee into our cellar if there is an emergency. All the other people in our area received the order to go to the school cellar when there is an air-raid warning. The substance of the school building is more resistant than that of the cellars in the flats, they say. I wonder if this is the real reason. Sadly, I have to tell you that the parcels will be smaller in the future because my deliveries are not so generous anymore, for many of the wealthier gentlemen are now at war also. Even my food is nearing the end. What I still have enough of are cigars, so everything is alright for your father. But all the same, I will send you as much as I can and this parcel has got the usual content. Please hug the children and greet your father.

Hugs,

Your Lilli

Letter from Erich to Eva 12th December 1943

My dear wife,

Everything is well here, as always. We had to withdraw a couple of times for tactical reasons and more comrades have died for the Führer. But as I have already told you, we have to make some more sacrifices before the final victory. But it is an honour. At the moment we are stationed in a small village where we did not need to build up our tents. During the winter it is warmer inside a house. But we don't even expect the Russian pigs to stay in such houses. Everything is crooked. Not to mention the nasty smell inside the houses. Our commander gave us the order to clean up first. He seems to hope that we can stay here over Christmas. We have enough fuel until then and if the fuel runs out we will use the furniture as fuel. It doesn't matter; we will burn everything anyway when we leave the place. We put our Jews into the barn. Three nights ago, Private Holz and I shot two of them during the guard duty when they tried to flee. We received a commendation for that. You and the children should be proud of me. I'm looking forward to staying with the comrades this Christmas. All leave is cancelled but I would have refused it anyway. In this important situation one has to be at the side of the comrades.

Is everything alright at home? Please greet Marie, Hildchen and the little ones from their father.

Kind regards,

Your husband Erich

Letter from Eva to Lilli 18th December 1943

Dear Lilli,

I'm very happy that your Hans is well. Even Erich is well; I just received a letter from him. Of course I'm happy when Erich is safe and sound but for a long time now it has given me no pleasure to read his letters. I'm sick and tired of the war. An explosive charge has torn off one of Rainer's legs, you know, Anna's husband. He is in the military hospital, it is uncertain if he will survive but as soon as he is fit for transportation he will be coming home.

Dear Lilli, I hope the war is over soon, regardless of who wins. It does not look good for us according to all I've heard and after what happened in Stalingrad. Although Erich always writes something else and on the radio they only talk about the final victory.

Lilli, your parcel embarrassed me. You wrote that your parcels are getting smaller but this one was the biggest you ever sent to us. I hid nearly everything to keep it for Christmas. Then we will eat caviar for the first time like the wealthy gentlemen. Sadly, I have to tell you it will probably be the last Christmas in our nice flat. The daughter of the landlord was bombed out in Hamburg and will now have our flat. I'm very desperate. I haven't told the children up until now but father says that we can move in with him, of course. He will then move in with Mrs Trapp until we have a new flat. Only one room and a kitchen. But what can I do? If it were not for this we would be out on the streets. It just has to work. I heard from a neighbour about the time bombs, which are often dropped over Hamburg. They lie around for hours before they explode. What a terrible idea. I hope you and your mother were spared. I pray for you. The children greet you very kindly and regards and thanks from father.

Hugs,

Your Eva

Diary entry 2nd October 1945

I was so afraid of it. Yesterday, Erich said it. He thinks it is no longer appropriate for me to sleep with one of the children in the bed. He demanded, now that he is well, that I, as his wife, sleep together with him. I did not know what to say. I tried to convince him it would be better for him to still have a bed of his own. But he interrupted me in a crude way and said that it has been decided, tonight I will sleep with him like I used to. How revolted I was by the idea of physical contact and how I hoped he would be too exhausted for that. He tried it but I resisted and the little ones woke up. Erich just shouted: "Quiet! Your mother is coming to you!"

Then he threw me out of the bed without a blanket and I had to spend the night in the bed and share the cover with the little ones. I preferred to be cold than to share one bed with him. This morning, Erich gave the big ones the order to put his bed into the kitchen again and the table and the chairs into our room: "So your mother and I have a bedroom of our own again", he said and he grinned at me. In this moment he was more disgusting than he had ever been before. He radiated not only hatred but also a violence, which he enjoyed. I'm afraid of tonight, I am more scared than I ever was during the war.

Lilli, if only you would get in touch.

Letter from Lilli to Eva 26th August 1944

Dear Eva,

It has happened. This is the beginning of the end, the shop and our flat are not there anymore. Everything destroyed with only one bomb. Mother and I were lucky. As always, we were at my mother's flat to fetch the post on Sunday when an alarm surprised us in broad daylight. We went to the bomb cellar in mother's district. There weren't many people; most of them probably thought that an alarm by daylight is only an exercise. But we were happy to be sat in the cellar as we heard the noise of the bombs far away. Shortly afterwards the all clear signal came and mother and I went to the shop. When we got out of the bus we could already see it. In front of the shop were several fire engines but I still had hope, for the front looked intact. But when I got nearer I knew. Nothing is left. The whole building has been burnt to cinders. Eva, our whole work was for nothing. Mother was so kind, she took me in her arms and we went straight back to her flat. She said that we were lucky; who knows whether we would have taken the alarm seriously if the shop were open. I know she is right, but...

This morning, I went to the shop again. I climbed over the blocks with the sign "Danger – building unsafe". Can you imagine, the way to the cellar was free. So I went into the cellar. It was like always. Apart from a few clefts and some broken pieces of the wall, everything was as if nothing had happened. I opened the cupboard, where the emergency reserves for the attacks were kept, with a key. Ten bars of chocolate, one box of pralines, seven tins of food, five bottles of lemonade and a bottle of brandy were left. Mother was really angry; she asked me what I would have done if everything had caved in. How could she have explained to Hans that I had lost my life through pure carelessness? She is right and I promised her not to go to the shop again. I decided not to write to Hans about it, I don't want to discourage him any further. He won't notice, for he sends his post to mother's address anyway. Sadly there won't be any more parcels. I hope you, the children and your father are well.

Hugs,

Your Lilli

Letter from Erich to Eva 27ᵗʰ August 1944

My dear wife,

We have had to withdraw further for a short time. The Russians are trying now to make us surrender through loudspeakers. Many of us are exhausted because there was near to no food in the last weeks and even the fuel ran out long ago. That's why some of us have lost their faith in this matter and due to this we had to shoot about a dozen deserters during the last two weeks. Sadly, one of them was private Bruns, with whom I blew up the dugout. But we are fighting for the final victory so we cannot make any exceptions. Now they have attempted to kill the Führer in order to steal the victory from us. Everyone says that the traitors were people paid by the Jews and the enemies. You can feel the excitement everywhere, the higher ranks are taking tough action against the smallest offences. That is good, maybe they should have done it before then we would have the victory already. Yesterday, we listened to a record of one of the speeches that the Führer gave. The sergeant told us that it was only recorded for the comrades in Russia. That made me proud again and made me believe even more in a victory for us. Please send me reserves and warm clothes.

Greet Marie, Hilde and the little ones from their father.
Kind regards,
Your husband, Erich
Heil Hitler

Diary entry 3ʳᵈ October 1945

Tonight he did it again, he said that it is my duty as his wife but I didn't want it, I'm so revolted by it. I resisted but he was stronger. Afterwards, I had to vomit but that didn't interest him, he just turned away and slept. I then went to the little ones in their bed. Even if I'm his wife and he is right, I hate him and I wish ... no, he is the father of my children. I have to bear it. I only hope that I will not become pregnant again.

Letter from Eva to Lilli 30th August 1944

Dear Lilli,

I cannot express how sorry I am. With one attack everything is destroyed. Hitler is to blame for it all with his war. I can't say how much I detest the war. Lilli, I'm sure that when the war is over that you will build up everything again, together with Hans. If someone has the power to do it then it's you, my dear Lilli. I know I can't comfort you but there is one thing I can do. Busloads of people are coming every day from Hamburg to exchange food here. Now that you haven't got a shop anymore, your mother and you probably aren't so well off so I will send you packages now, for here it is far easier to organise something. Even father and Lieselotte have contributed something to the package. Lieselotte made the cake. Father sends you his remaining cigars, he says that you can maybe trade one thing or the other for them. Kind regards from him and we all agree that if you and your mother can't stand it anymore in the city then you can stay with us. You with me and the children and your mother could have a bed in Lieselotte's kitchen. We would be happy to have you with us.

Certainly it is safer here than in the city, even though a lost plane dropped bombs here twice. I think you are so courageous for not telling Hans about your disaster and for bearing all the loss alone. I hope Hans is well.

Erich wrote that he is well. The war appears to be nearing the end according to how he has described it. Violence is increasing. Reading his letters frightens me. I'm glad to be here with the children. The only thing I can do is write letters to him but even this has become difficult for me. I wish the war was over.

I must greet you from everyone here. The children insisted that I send you a big kiss from them.

Hugs,

Your Eva

Letter from Lilli to Eva 17th September 1944

Dear Eva,

How happy I was about your letter and your package. And you are wrong; nothing has comforted me more than your letter. I talked with mother for long time about your offer but mother does not want to leave Hamburg, despite the fact that we have to go into the cellar every night and that our food reserves are not sufficient. So I am going to stay here with her, of course. I may have already found a way to improve our situation. I called the high member of the party, who saved my car. You need to know that he still likes to celebrate regularly. Unbelievable in this situation. But it means for me that he has arranged for platters to be delivered to mother's flat tomorrow. He has also arranged for some suppliers to give me small amounts of food, even though I no longer have a shop. His only condition was that the empty platters have to stand prepared and ready in his flat on Saturday evening. That is a start. Perhaps there is someone else at this celebration who wants to have a party and needs my platters too. At least on Saturday mother and I can eat till we are full again and there will presumably be a little left over. You see, luck hasn't left me completely. The only thing missing is a letter from Hans, the last one came a long time ago. But I hope for the best. Please give the children a big kiss and greet your father and Mrs Trapp and pass my kind thanks on to them for their generous offer.

My dear Eva, affectionately,

Your Lilli

Letter from Eva to Lilli 1st October 1944

Dear Lilli,

I'm so happy about your new beginning. You simply never give up. I'm so different. How I would love to have your courage. I always adored you for that. You just go and ask the high gentlemen. That was always your way, even during the time when we lived together in the shoe shop. It is so long ago. Perhaps there will be such nice times for us again after the war. But at the moment I am worrying a great deal. I haven't heard from Erich for a long time. He didn't answer my last three letters. I am already fearing the worst. It got worse when I got my last three letters back, tied together in a bundle, from the postman yesterday. In this moment it was clear to me that Erich has fallen. But then I read the stamp on the letters and couldn't believe it: "Addressee not available, Addressee is wanted because of abandonment of the unit."

I couldn't believe that Erich had abandoned the army. But today I became certain about it. This morning at nine o'clock, there were two soldiers at the front door. They were very polite. They said they are military policemen and that they have to search the flat for lance corporal Erich Kummer, who left unauthorized. When they did not find him, they asked me whether I knew where lance corporal Erich Kummer is staying at the moment. I told them the truth, of course. Because they were so friendly I also added that I just couldn't believe that Erich had done such a thing. That's what they hear again and again, they said. Then they told me that Erich fled during guard duty and before that he stole the food reserves of three comrades, a pair of boots and a pair of socks. Then they warned me that the hiding of a deserter is treason to the Führer and the fatherland and that the punishment, as it is for abandonment, is the death penalty. That didn't scare me much, but Erich as a deserter? He, who always believed in the final victory? Lilli, I don't know what to think, I mean if the war is over soon then he may survive. Is there a possibility to fight one's way back from Russia? And if so, is he on his way here? His food reserves won't last long. I was relieved actually. Erich is alive, but you know, I wept for he has betrayed his comrades. He would never have done such thing before the war. Lilli, what is the war turning us into? I didn't tell the children the truth. When they asked me, I said their father has written that he is well, as always.

How was your first delivery and are there new orders, was there something left? We packed up a small parcel with the essentials, just in case. Kind regards from the children and from father.

Hugs

Yours Eva

Letter from Lilli to Eva 4ᵗʰ October 1944

Dear Eva,

Your news is rather surprising. I cannot tell if it is good news or bad news. Concerning Erich's behaviour; I wouldn't fret about it. Who knows whether the two of them told the truth? But you are right in one point; war brings many of our bad sides to light. I had to think about poor Mrs Rosenthal when I read your words. I wasn't courageous enough to offer her a hiding place. The only thing that comforts me in this matter is the fact that if I had done it, she presumably would have been bombed out with her children in my flat. But for me it is only a cold comfort. Life goes on, how often I have heard these words when the customers told me about their personal war tragedies. But it is true.

My order was a success in every respect. I received all the sorts of food that I ordered and the platters were accepted very well. I have two orders for next week and in two weeks I even have three. But the most important thing is that I could take the remains and some of the products that weren't open home with me. That's why I am sending your parcel back. Many thanks, the first parcel really helped us but this one is more important for you. If it carries on as it is now then we needn't worry. I even added a few things to the parcel. Among other

126

things, I added the cigars, which your father sent us. I didn't have the
time to change them and now I don't need them anymore. Please
greet him and give the children a kiss from me.
Hugs,
Your Lilli

Letter from Eva to Lilli 2nd December 1944

Dear Lilli,
It is so terrible, I don't know what to do. Father is dead. Can you come
here? Please. I cannot understand it, bombs have only been dropped
here three times. And straight away the first one, which hit its target,
kills him. It was this morning at four o'clock. He was in the bakery as
usual and then a bomb hit the house. They are all dead. Father, the
old baker woman and two of her grandchildren, who have helped in
the bakery since their father was called to war. Think of the mother,
how shall she cope, what should she tell her husband at the front? It
is so cruel. And everybody came to me. Anna is unable to
communicate, she screamed like a mad woman. I had to hold her the
whole time and couldn't care for the children. How thankful I am that
Lieselotte was so brave, she had the energy to comfort the children.
Now they are all sitting in the next room and it is somehow quiet. I'm
sitting in the kitchen. Lilli, please come, I need you; he was so fond of
you.
Hugs,
Your Eva

Letter from Lilli to Eva 20th December 1944

Dear Eva,
How are you? Two weeks have passed since the funeral. I think it was
one of the most touching moments of my life. I have never told you
this but I had somehow adopted your father a little bit. I always

pretended that he was my father too. And he always treated me a little bit like a daughter. He was so glad when I visited, he always asked questions about Hans-Georg, the shop and even about mother. He was really interested in me. He was such a wonderful man. I felt the Pastor was very courageous when he openly blamed the war and those who provoked it for the death of your father. You mentioned that the two of them were friends. If your father was listening from a better world, which I hope for more and more, he would have been content. Despite this occasion, those two days were the saddest but also the nicest days of the war. Since our time together in Hamburg it was the first time that we have spent so much time together. And to be together with the children for such a long time was very nice too, even if it made me realize what I will never have. That made me especially sad on my way home. But by the time that I had reached mother's house again the gratefulness for having you and the children was predominant. The way home was hard, I had to let troops pass by again and again. Once, I drove over a bomb crater on the street, which wasn't there on the way to you, and only two planks were laid over it. I hope so much that Hans and Erich come back from the last stretches of war alive. It cannot last much longer. Please hug the children from me. I nearly wrote 'parcel as always'. I, too, have to learn that he is not there anymore. I am thinking of you.

Hugs,

Your Lilli

Letter from Eva to Lilli 14th January 1945

Dear Lilli,

The daily routine seems to have returned. The children didn't want to sleep at all the first nights after father's death. They all came to me again and again and wept bitterly. But now they're sleeping again as usual. They're going to school and doing their homework, talking about their little quarrels and about their friends. Even Anna has got a grip on herself again, although some bad news came for her last week. Rainer died from his wounds. I heard it first from our postman, he recognises such envelopes. So I went to her at once. I was very worried. But she was composed, she told me that Rainer hadn't written to her once from the front and that she gave it up after half a year. She never talked about it but she wasn't able to forgive him for the last conflicts that they had. Honestly, Lilli, she looked almost relieved. I don't think we can imagine what it is like to have such a heavy drinker as a husband. She didn't even want to have his belongings. On the same day she traded her wedding ring for food at the market. She sent his fob watch to Rainer's brother's wife in Köln. Dear Lilli, many thanks for the parcel. I assume that my children are the only ones in the village who can still regularly eat chocolate. Many hugs from them. I hope you and your mother are well and that your deal with the platters is still working well.

Hugs,

Your Eva

Letter from Johannes Huber to Lilli 22nd April 1945

Dear Mrs Marten,

We don't know each other, although you sent such generous parcels to my dear wife. Unfortunately, I am writing for a sad reason. I have to tell you that your husband was seriously injured by a piece of shrapnel during an attack by the Russians yesterday. I brought him, together with comrade Jung, behind the lines at once. There he was looked after. This morning, it was decided to bring him together with other wounded to a casualty clearing station far behind the lines, for it is not certain for how long we can keep this sector. I heard that some of the wounded comrades were brought as far as Berlin. The lucky ones. Perhaps Hans-Georg is one of those. But I want to stay truthful; the wound on his shoulder- and neck area does not look good to me. I hope the best for you and Hans-Georg. He has become a true friend of mine.

Kind   regards,
Johannes Huber

Diary entry 5th October 1945

Tonight, I refused to do it. I kicked him right into his ... He convulsed with pain. I then fled into our room to the children. He didn't follow me. But the next morning was terrible. He hit Marie because of nothing. When the children were at school he said that if I don't want him to take his anger out on the children that I shouldn't do such thing like last night ever again. How can he be so cruel? What kind of man has he become?

Letter from Lilli to Eva 1st May 1945

Dear Eva,

Maybe it has to be that way; one piece of good news is caught up by a bad one. I heard about Hitler's death this morning on the radio. Suicide? If it is true, it would be fitting for this monster. Rushing countless people into a war and then committing suicide; when there is nothing to win anymore to flee from responsibility. However, it seems as if he is really dead this time. But sadly, the consequences of his deeds are not over yet. The war is still not over and Hans-Georg is one of those who were hit. He is badly injured. Johannes Huber, one of his comrades, wrote to me and told me that Hans is on his way to a military hospital but he does not know where. If he is lucky then he will end up in Berlin. I didn't know what to do, I would have loved to drive there at once. Mother stopped me. She said that I wouldn't get to Berlin that way and that I don't really know whether he will even be taken to Berlin. Of course she was right and after I got over the first shock I went directly to the high member of the party, you know the one who helped me with the car. He said that it may be the last thing that he can do. Then he asked me a lot of questions, which rank Hans had, where he was stationed, when he was taken to hospital. After that he left me alone in his reception room. It took over an hour until he returned. But the waiting was worthwhile. The most important thing was that he could confidently say that Hans was still alive this morning. The train which was transporting the injured started the next stage of its journey then. He couldn't find out where they are at the moment. The area is extremely dangerous and one cannot say where the Russians are already and which way the train has gone. The train has received the orders to bring the wounded to Berlin and to avoid all areas which are under fire. He then underlined again that this is not easy. He also couldn't find out why these wounded, out of all of them, should be brought to Berlin. He assumed that there must be some high party members among them. When I told him that I am going to drive to Berlin he laughed and made it clear to me that I would never reach my destination without the right permits. He managed to get those for me as well, after I had waited for another two hours. Anyway, when he returned I had everything that I needed. Yet he tried to convince me to not go to Berlin, regardless of the route I would take. The area around Berlin is suffering from constant bombings. And the nearer the Russians come, the worse it will get.

But you know me. So, dear Eva, when you receive this letter I will be on my way. Mother has packed a large rucksack with food reserves for me. And I took some of mother's jewellery and father's golden fob watch, in case I can't go on my way with my permits. Eva, pray for me. Until today it was not clear to me how much I love Hans-Georg. I always thought he loves me more than I do him. How wrong I was. I'll be in touch as soon as possible. Please kiss the children from me. Hugs,

Your Lilli

Diary entry 7th October 1945

Lilli, you have been missing for six months now. Where are you? How I would love to talk to you about all my sufferings. He forces me to do it every night. It is so repulsive. But I don't have to vomit anymore. I stay with him afterwards too. I don't want to wake up the children every night. It is so terrible for me but he is no longer so violent. He sometimes even starts to talk with the children about their friends and what they like to do. Sometimes he comes into the kitchen and sits beside them for a short time when they do their homework. Once, he even helped the little ones with a sum. He could do sums very well, as he was responsible for farmer Ranfts' accounts. All the same, the children are still afraid of him and I have urged them not to speak about the war or the time before the war when he is present. It is all getting better, apart from the feelings that I have towards him. I hope that they will get better too.

Letter from Lilli's mother to Eva 14th October 1945

Dear Eva,

It is my sad duty to inform you about Lilli's death. This morning, I received the letter. It bears a stamp from the last days of the war. Lilli was hit by a rifle bullet in Berlin on 5th May. She was identified by her passport. The captain who told me about Lilli's death also informed me that she was buried in due form at the cemetery, Berlin-Zehlendorf. He, as an office worker, took part in the funeral. The costs for the funeral, the grave and the wooden cross, were paid for using public funds. I will receive a bill soon. Dear Eva, Lilli would have certainly laughed about the bureaucracy a few days before the end of the war. Lilli has kept all your letters safe and she gave me the order before she left to send all the letters to you if she were to be hurt. She

thought they would be safe at your place. I sadly don't have any
information about Hans-Georg's whereabouts.
Grieving deeply,
Your Katrin Hartwig

Diary entry 17th October 1945

Lilli is dead. For whom I have written everything down? Who will comfort me now or give me advice?

The children shall not find out what I think. Lilli is dead. There is no sense in writing anymore. I will throw everything into the oven. Everything remains as it is; I have to endure him for the children. So much violence, the war is responsible for that, I hate him. I hate Erich.

Letter from Lilli's mother to Eva 25th November 1945

Dear Eva,

I can inform you now about the whereabouts of Hans-Georg. Today, I received a letter from a home. Lilli's address was on the letter. Hans-Georg is in a home for disabled veterans. He, sadly, has not only lost his left arm because of his serious injury, but also his reason. The doctor, who wrote this letter for Lilli, says he lives in a sort of dream world. He utters disconnected sentences and seems to notice nothing around him. Only when he hears her name does he shortly seem to see his surroundings. But this state only lasts for a few seconds.

She urgently asks Lilli in her letter to visit, for this may help him to recover. I have just informed her about Lilli's death. Maybe it is better for Hans-Georg if he does not notice anything. He loved Lilli terribly.
Yours sincerely,
Katrin Hartwig

Diary entry 12th March 1956

Erich is dead. I don't feel anything. No grief, no anger, not even pity.

Diary entry 20th March 1956

Today, I visited Lilli's grave. I found the wooden cross quickly. I finally read the diary to her and said goodbye. How much I still miss her.

Last diary entry 21st March 1956

Today, I fetched Hans-Georg from the home. He hasn't changed a bit. Even his hair hasn't turned grey. I don't think he recognised me at first. He was so far away. Only at Lilli's grave did that change. I told him that Lilli is lying there. Then he looked at me and then at the wooden cross and read aloud: "Lilli Marten, born Hartwig."

After that he cried like a child. I embraced him and held him. But suddenly he turned me away and looked at me with his absent eyes. But I'm sure he understood.

Frank Salewski

Der Tag,
an dem der
Schmetterling
starb

Roman

KILLROY *media*